THE BABYLONIAN MASK

ORDER OF THE BLACK SUN SERIES - BOOK 14

PRESTON WILLIAM CHILD

Edited (USA) by Usnea Lebendig

Where is the sense in the senses when there is no face?

Where walks the Blind when there is but dark and holes, empty?

Where speaks the Heart without the release by tongue the lips to fare?

Where tracks the sweet scent of roses and lover's breath when absent lies smell?

How will I tell?

How will I tell?

What hide they behind their masks

When their faces are secret and their voices compel?

Do they hold Heaven?

Or do they wield Hell?

~ Masque de Babel (circa 1682 - Versailles)

1

THE BURNING MAN

*N*ina blinked profusely. Her eyes listened to her synapses as her slumber fell into REM, abandoning her to the cruel talons of her subconscious mind. In the private ward of the University Hospital of Heidelberg, the lights buzzed through the dead of night where Dr. Nina Gould had been admitted to reverse, if possible, the dreaded effects of radiation sickness. So far, it had been difficult to diagnose how critical her case really was, as the man who'd accompanied her had inaccurately relayed her level of exposure. The best he could say was that he'd found her wandering the underground tunnels of Chernobyl a few hours too long for any living creature to recover.

"He did not tell us everything," affirmed Sister Barken to her small group of subordinates, "but I had a distinct inkling it was not half of what Dr. Gould had endured down there before he claimed to have found her." She shrugged and sighed. "Unfortunately, short of arresting him for a crime we do not have any proof of, we had to let him go and deal with the little information we had."

Obligatory sympathy played on the faces of the trainees, but they were only masking the boredom of the night behind professional guises. Their young blood sang for the freedom of the pub, where the group usually met after their shifts together or for the embraces of their lovers at this time of night. Sister Barken did not tolerate their double entendres and missed the company of her peers, where she could exchange actual cogent verdicts with those equally qualified and passionate about medicine.

Her protruding eyeballs combed them, one by one, as she imparted Dr. Gould's condition. Slanting at the corners, her thin lips fell downward in an implication of discontent that she often mirrored in her harsh, low tone when she spoke. Apart from being a stern veteran of the German medical practice adhered to at the Heidelberg Uni, she was also known to be quite the brilliant diagnostician. It was a surprise to her colleagues that she never bothered to further her career by becoming a physician, or even a resident consultant.

"What is the nature of her circumstances, Sister Barken?" asked a young nurse, shocking the Sister with a show of actual interest. The fifty-year-old buxom superior took a moment to answer, looking almost happy to have been asked the question instead of having to stare into the comatose gaze of entitled runts all night.

"Well, that was all we could find out from the German gentleman who brought her in, Nurse Marx. We could find no corroboration as to the cause of her illness, save that which the man told us." She sighed, frustrated by the lack of background pertaining to Dr. Gould's state. "All I can say is that she seems to have been rescued in time to be treated.

Although she exhibits all the signs of acute poisoning, her system seems to be able to combat it satisfactorily...for now."

Nurse Marx nodded, ignoring the scoffing reaction of her colleagues. It intrigued her. After all, she had heard much of this Nina Gould from her mother. At first, by the way she babbled on about her, she had thought her mother actually knew the petite Scottish historian. It didn't take long, however, for medical student Marlene Marx to find out that her mother was simply an avid reader of the journals and two books published by Gould. Thus, Nina Gould was a bit of a celebrity in her house.

Was this another of the clandestine excursions the historian had undertaken, like those she had lightly touched on in her books? Marlene often wondered why Dr. Gould did not write more about her adventures with the well-known explorer and inventor from Edinburgh, David Purdue, but rather hinted upon the many journeys. Then there was the well-accounted association with the world-renowned investigative journalist, Sam Cleave, that Dr. Gould had written about. Not only did Marlene's mom speak of Nina as if she were a friend of the family, but speculated about her life as if the feisty historian were a walking soap opera.

It was only a matter of time before Marlene's mother would start reading books about or published by Sam Cleave himself, if only to find out more about the other rooms in the great Gould mansion. All this mania was precisely why the nurse had been keeping Gould's stay at Heidelberg a secret, fearing her mother would stage a one-woman march into the west wing of the 14th Century medical facility in protest to her captivity or something. It made Marlene smile to herself, but at the risk of provoking the carefully avoided anger of Sister Barken, she hid her amusement.

The group of medical students did not know about the creeping convoy of injury approaching the emergency room a floor below. Under their feet a team of orderlies and night staff nurses were surrounding a screaming young man who was refusing to be strapped to a gurney.

"Please, sir, you have to stop screaming!" the head nurse on duty begged the man as she cordoned off his furious path of destruction with her rather large frame. Her eyes flashed toward one of the male nurses armed with a shot of succinylcholine surreptitiously approaching the burn victim. The horrible sight of the wailing man had two of the newer staff members gagging, barely composing themselves as they waited for the head nurse to shout her next order. For most of them, however, this was a typical panic scenario, although every circumstance was different. They had, for instance, never had a burn victim *running* into the ER before, let alone one that was still exuding smoke as he skidded, losing clumps of flesh from his chest and abdomen along the way.

Thirty five seconds felt like two hours for the stumped German medical professionals. Soon after the big woman cornered the victim with the blackened head and chest, the screams halted abruptly, changing into rasps of choking.

"Airway edema!" she roared in a powerful voice that could be heard throughout the emergency ward. "Intubation, now!"

The stalking male nurse lunged forward, planting a needle in the asphyxiating man's crisp skin and pushing the plunger without reservation. He winced as the syringe crackled through the epidermis of the poor patient, but it had to be done.

"Christ! That smell is sickening!" one of the nurses huffed under her breath to her colleague, who nodded in agreement. They covered their faces momentarily to catch their breath as the stench of cooked flesh assaulted their senses. It was not very professional, but they were only people after all.

"Get him to O.R. *'B'*!" the robust lady thundered to her staff. "Schnell! He is in cardiac arrest, people! Move!" They fitted an oxygen mask on the convulsing patient as his coherence waned. Nobody noticed the tall, old man in the black coat on his trail. His long, stretching shadow darkened the pristine door glass where he stood watching the smoking carcass being wheeled away. Under the brim of his fedora his green eyes glinted and his wasted lips sneered in defeat.

With all of the chaos in the emergency room, he knew he would not be noticed and slipped through the doors to haunt the ground floor locker room a few feet past the reception area. Once inside the locker room he escaped detection by eluding the bright luminescence of the small ceiling lights above the benches. As it was the middle of night shift, there would not likely be any medical staff in the changing room, so he procured a pair of scrubs and made for the showers. In one of the obscured cubicles the old man shed his clothing.

Under the tiny, circular lights above him, his skeletal, powdery form revealed itself in the reflection in the Plexiglas. Grotesque and gaunt, his elongated limbs shook off his suit and sheathed themselves in the cotton scrubs. His laden breath wheezed as he moved, mimicking a robotic, skin-wearing android pumping hydraulic fluid through its joints during every shift. When he removed his fedora to replace it with the scrub cap, his deformed skull mocked him in the mirror image of the Plexiglas. Each dent and protrusion of his skull was accentuated by the angle of the light, but he kept his head bowed as much as he could during the fitting of the cap. He did not want to be confronted by his biggest handicap, his mightiest deformity – his facelessness.

Only his eyes were evident of his human countenance, perfectly shaped, but lonely in their normality. The old man did not suffer himself the indignity of his own reflection's mockery, where his cheekbones flanked a featureless face. Hardly any hole formed between his nearly absent lips and above his meager mouth, and only two tiny fissures served as nostrils. The last piece of his clever disguise would be the surgical mask, elegantly finishing off his ruse.

Shoving his suit into the farthest cabinet on the east wall and just pushing the narrow door shut, he corrected his posture.

"Abend," he muttered.

He shook his head. No, his dialect was wrong. He cleared his throat and took a moment to collect his thoughts. "Abend." No. Again. "Ah-bent," he enunciated more clearly and listened to his hoarse voice. The accent was almost there; only one or two more tries.

"Abend," he spoke clearly and loudly as the door to the locker room swung open. Too late. He held his breath to break the word.

"Abend, Herr Doctor," the entering male nurse smiled as he

6

proceeded to the adjacent room to hit the urinals. "Wie geht's?"

"Gut, gut," the old man replied hastily, relieved at the nurse's oblivion. He cleared his throat and headed for the door. It was growing late in the hour and he still had unfinished business to attend to regarding the smoking hot new arrival.

Feeling almost ashamed of the animal method he used to track down the young man he had followed to the emergency room, he tilted his head back and sniffed the air. That familiar odor compelled him to trail it like a shark would relentlessly follow blood through miles of water. He paid little attention to the courteous greetings of staff, janitors and night doctors. Without a sound, his covered feet trod step after step as he obeyed the acute scent of burning flesh and disinfectant where it was strongest in his nostrils.

"*Zimmer 4*," he mumbled as his nose led him left at a t-junction of hallways. He would have smiled – if he could. His thin body crept down the burn unit hallway to where the young man was being treated. From the inside of the room he could hear the voices of the doctor and nurses declare the patient's chances of survival.

"He will live, although," the male doctor sighed sympathetically, "I don't think he will be able to retain his facial functions – features, yes, but his sense of smell and taste will be permanently severely impaired."

"He still has a face under all that, doctor?" a nurse asked softly.

"Yes, but barely, as the skin damage will cause his features to...well...dissolve into the face a bit more. His nose will not be prominent and his lips," he hesitated, feeling truly sorry for the attractive young man on the barely intact driver's license in the charred wallet, "are gone. Poor child. Barely twenty-seven and this happens to him."

The doctor shook his head almost imperceptibly. "Administer some IV analgesics and start urgent fluid replacement please, Sabine."

"Yes, doctor." She sighed and helped her colleague collect the dressing. "He will have to wear a mask for the rest of his life," she said to no one in particular. She pulled the trolley closer, carrying the sterile bandages and saline solution. They did not see the alien presence of the intruder peering in from the hallway, finding his target through the slowly closing slit in the door. Only one word escaped him silently.

"Mask."

2

STEALING PURDUE

*F*eeling somewhat concerned, Sam strolled casually through the vast garden of the private institution just outside Dundee under a roaring Scottish sky. After all, was there any other kind? He felt good, though, inside himself. Empty. So much had befallen him and his friends of late that it felt amazing to think of nothing, for a change. Sam had returned from Kazakhstan a week before and had not laid eyes on either Nina or Purdue since he had returned to Edinburgh.

He had been informed that Nina had suffered serious injuries due to radiation exposure and had been admitted to a hospital in Germany. After he had sent new acquaintance Detlef Holtzer to find her, he had remained in Kazakhstan for a few days and had not been able to obtain any updates on Nina's condition. Apparently Dave Purdue had also been discovered at the same site as Nina, only to be subdued by Detlef for his strangely aggressive behavior. But that also was speculative at best, thus far.

Purdue had contacted Sam himself the day before to notify

him of his own confinement in the *Sinclair Medical Research Facility*. Funded and managed by the *Brigade Apostate*, the Sinclair Medical Research Facility was a clandestine ally of Purdue's in a past battle against the Order of the Black Sun. The association happened to be ex-members of the Black Sun; apostates of the faith, so to speak, that Sam had also become a member of a few years earlier. His operations for them were few and far between, as their need for intelligence would surface only every now and then. Being a sharp and efficient investigative journalist, Sam Cleave was invaluable to the Brigade in this regard.

Other than the latter, he was free to operate in his own capacity and do his own freelance work whenever he felt like it. Weary of doing anything as intense as his last mission any time soon, Sam had elected to take the time to visit Purdue in whatever madhouse the eccentric explorer had checked into this time.

There was very little information on the Sinclair Facility, but Sam had a nose for smelling the meat under the lid. As he approached the place, he noticed that there were bars on the windows all across the third floor of the four stories the building boasted.

"I bet you are in one of those rooms, hey, Purdue?" Sam chuckled to himself as he proceeded toward the grand entrance to the creepy building with its overly white walls. A chill ran through Sam as he entered the lobby. "Geez, Hotel California posing as the Stanley much?"

"Good morning," the petite, blond receptionist greeted Sam. Her smile was genuine. His rugged, dark looks instantly intrigued her, even if he were old enough to be her much older brother or almost too old uncle.

"Aye, that it is, young lady," Sam agreed flamboyantly. "I am here to see David Purdue."

She frowned, "Then who is the bouquet for, sir?"

Sam just winked and tilted his right hand downward to hide the flower arrangement under the counter. "Shh, don't tell him. He hates carnations."

"Um," she stuttered in abject uncertainty, "he is in Ward 3, up two floors, Room 309."

"Ta," Sam grinned and whistled as he walked toward the staircase that was marked in white and green – '*Ward 2, Ward 3, Ward 4,*' swinging his bouquet lazily as he ascended. In the mirror he was greatly amused by the trailing stare of the bewildered young woman who was still trying to figure out what the flowers were for.

"Aye, just as I thought," Sam mumbled as he found the hallway to the right of the landing where 'Ward 3' was marked on a similarly uniform green and white sign. "The loony floor with the bars and Purdue is the mayor."

In no way did the place resemble a hospital, really. It looked more like a conglomerate of medical offices and practices in a large mall, but Sam had to admit that he found the lack of expected lunacy just a tad unsettling. Nowhere did he see people in white hospital gowns, or wheelchairs transporting the half-dead and dangerous. Even the medical staff, which he could only tell apart by the white coats, looked remarkably serene and casual.

They would nod and greet him cordially as he passed them, not making a single inquiry into the flowers he had in his hand. Such acceptance just took the fun out of Sam's intended humor and he dumped the bouquet into a nearby trash bin just before he reached the allocated room. The door was closed, of course, being on the barred floor, yet Sam was dumbstruck when he found that it was unlocked. Even more astonishing was the interior of the room.

Apart from one well-draped window and two posh luxury seats, there was little else but a carpet. His dark eyes scrutinized the strange room. It was missing a bed and the privacy of an en suite bathroom. Staring out the window, Purdue sat with his back to Sam.

"So glad you came, old boy," he said in the same cheerful, richer-than-God tone he usually used to address his guests at his mansion.

"Pleasure," Sam replied, still trying to solve the conundrum of the furniture. Purdue turned to face him, looking healthy and relaxed.

"Sit down," he invited the stumped journalist, who seemed to be investigating the room for bugs or hidden explosives, by the look on his face. Sam sat down. "So," Purdue started, "where are my flowers?"

Sam gawked at Purdue. "I thought *I* was the one with the mind control thing?"

Purdue looked unperturbed by Sam's declaration, something they both knew but neither supported. "No, I saw you saunter up the drive with it in your hand, no doubt bought just to embarrass me in some way or another."

"God, you are getting to know me too well," Sam sighed. "But how can you see anything past the maximum security bars here? I noticed that the inmates' cells are left unlocked.

What is the point of barring you in if they keep your doors open?"

Purdue, amused, smiled and shook his head. "Oh, it is not to keep us from escaping, Sam. It is to keep us from jumping." It was the first time a bitter and snide tone had haunted Purdue's voice. Sam picked up on his friend's unease, coming to the fore in the ebb and flow of his self-control. It appeared that Purdue's apparent tranquility was just a mask over this uncharacteristic discontent.

"Are you prone to such a thing?" asked Sam.

Purdue shrugged. "I don't know, Master Cleave. One moment all is well and the next I am back in that bloody exaggerated fish tank, wishing I could drown faster than that ink fish swallowing my brain."

At once Purdue's expression had gone from a sunny silliness to an alarmingly pallid depression, brimming with guilt and worry. Sam dared to lay his hand on Purdue's shoulder, having no idea how the billionaire was going to react. But Purdue did nothing as Sam's hand comforted his turmoil.

"Is that what you are doing here? Trying to reverse the brainwashing that fuckwit Nazi subjected you to?" Sam asked him blatantly. "But that is good, Purdue. How are you progressing with the treatment? You seem your old self in most ways."

"Do I?" Purdue sneered. "Sam, do you know what it is like to not know? It is worse than knowing, I can assure you. But I have found that knowing breeds a different demon than being oblivious to one's actions."

"How do you mean?" Sam frowned. "I take it some actual

memories have returned; things you could not recall before?"

Purdue's pale blue eyes stared through the clean lenses of his glasses, straight ahead into space as he considered Sam's opinion before explaining. He looked almost maniacal in the darkening light of the cloudy weather that spilled through the window. His long, slender fingers fiddled with the carvings on the chair's wooden armrest as he dazed away. Sam thought it well to change the subject for the moment.

"So what the hell is with there being no bed?" he exclaimed, looking back at the mostly empty room.

"I never sleep."

That was all.

That was all Purdue had to say on the matter. His lack of elaboration unnerved Sam, because it was the antithesis of the man's trademark behavior. Usually he would cast aside all propriety or inhibition and spew out a grand tale filled with *what* and *why* and *who*. Now he was content with just the fact, so Sam pried, not only to force Purdue to explain, but because he genuinely wanted to know. "You know that is biologically impossible, unless you want to die in a fit of psychosis."

The look Purdue gave him made Sam's skin crawl. It was halfway between insane and perfectly happy; the look on a feral animal being fed, if Sam had to guess. His gray-soiled blond hair was painfully neat as always, combed back in long strands away from his grey sideburns. Sam imagined Purdue with unkempt hair in the communal showers, those pale blues piercing the guards' as they discovered him chewing at someone's ear. What bothered him most was how unremarkable such a scenario suddenly seemed for the state his friend was in. Purdue's words snapped Sam out of his hideous pondering.

"And what do you think is sitting right here in front of you, old cock?" Purdue sniggered, looking rather ashamed of his condition under the drooping grin he had tried to keep upbeat with. "This is what psychosis looks like, not that Hollywood overacting bollocks where people tear their hair out and write their names in shit on the walls. It is a silent thing, a silent creeping cancer that make you not care about the things you have to do to stay alive anymore. You are left alone with your thoughts and your deeds without a thought for eating..." He looked back at the bare patch of carpet where the bed was supposed to be, "...sleeping. At first my body caved under the robbery of rest. Sam, you should have seen me. Frantic and exhausted I would pass out on the floor." He shifted closer to Sam. Alarmingly the journalist could smell medical spirits and old cigarettes on Purdue's breath.

"Purdue..."

"No, no, you asked. Now you l-listen, al-alright?" Purdue insisted in a whisper. "I have not slept in over four days straight now and you know what? I feel great! I mean, look at me. Don't I look the picture of health?"

"That is what concerns me, pal," Sam winced, scratching his head. Purdue laughed. It was not a crazy cackle by any means, but a civilized, gentle chuckle. Purdue swallowed his amusement to whisper, "You know what I think?"

"That I'm not really here?" Sam guessed. "God knows this

bland and boring place would make me question reality in a big way."

"No. No. I think when I was brainwashed by the Black Sun they somehow removed my need for sleep. They must have reprogrammed my brain...un-unlocked...that primitive power they used on super soldiers back in World War II to make animals of men. They did not fall when shot, Sam. They kept walking, on and on and on..."

"Fuck this. I'm getting you out of here," Sam decided.

"I have not reached my full term reversal, Sam. Let me stay and let them erase all the atrocious behaviorisms," Purdue insisted, trying to sound reasonable and mentally sound, when all he wanted to do was to break out of the facility and run back to his home at Wrichtishousis.

"You say that," Sam dismissed in a clever tone, "but you don't mean it."

He pulled Purdue out of his chair. The billionaire smiled at his rescuer, looking decidedly elated. "You definitely still have the mind control thing."

3

THE SHAPE WITH BAD WORDS

*N*ina woke up, feeling poorly yet perceiving her surroundings vividly. It was the first time she had awoken without being roused by the sound of a nurse's voice or a doctor feeling the urge to administer a dosage at ungodly hours of the morning. It had always fascinated her how nurses always woke patients to give them 'something to sleep' at ridiculous hours, often between two and five in the morning. The logic of such practices eluded her completely, and she made no secret of her vexation for such idiocy, regardless of the explanations offered for it. Her body ached under the sadistic thrall of the radiation poisoning, but she tried to bear it for as long as she could.

To her relief, she'd learned from the on-duty physician that the sporadic burn wounds to her skin would heal in time, and that the exposure she had suffered under ground zero at Chernobyl was remarkably minor for such a hazardous area. Nausea would trouble her daily until the antibiotics had run their course, at least, but her hematopoietic presentation was still of great concern to him.

Nina understood his concern for the damage to her autoimmune system, but for her there were worse scars – both emotional and physical. She could not focus very well since she'd been liberated from the tunnels. It was unclear if it was caused by prolonged visual inactivity from the hours spent in practically pitch darkness, or if it was also the work of her exposure to high concentrations of old nuclear waves. Regardless, her emotional injury manifested in worse ways than the physical pain and skin blisters.

Nightmares plagued her about the way Purdue hunted her in the dark. Reliving small shards of recollection, her dreams would remind her of the groans he'd uttered after he laughed wickedly somewhere in the hellish blackness of the Ukrainian netherworld they'd been trapped in together. Through the other IV tube, sedatives kept her mind locked in the dreams, unable to fully awake to escape them. It was a subliminal torment she could not communicate to the scientifically-minded people who were only concerned with alleviating her physical ailments. They had no time to waste on her impending insanity.

Outside her window the pale threat of dawn winked, although the whole world was still sleeping around her. Faintly she could hear the low tones and whispers exchanged between medical staff, interspersed with the odd clink of teacups and coffee furnaces. It reminded Nina of very early mornings during school holidays when she was a wee girl in Oban. Her parents and mum's dad would whisper just like that as they gathered up the camping gear for the trip to the Hebrides. They would try not to wake little Nina while they packed the cars and only at the very end would her dad steal into her room, gather her up in her blankets like a hotdog roll, and carry her into the freezing morning air to put her into the backseat.

It was a fond memory she now briefly revisited in much the same way. Two nurses entered her room to check her drip and change the linen on the empty bed opposite hers. Even though they were talking in hushed tones, Nina was able to employ her knowledge of German to eavesdrop, just like those mornings when her family thought she was sound asleep. Keeping still and breathing deeply through her nose, Nina managed to fool the shift sister into believing she was fast asleep.

"How is she doing?" the nurse asked her superior, as she roughly rolled up the old sheet she'd pulled off the empty mattress.

"Her vitals are good," the head sister answered softly.

"What I was saying was that they should have dressed his skin with more Flamazine before fitting his mask. I think I am correct in suggesting it. There was no reason for Dr. Hilt to bite my head off," the nurse complained about an incident Nina reckoned the two had been discussing since before they came to check on her.

"You know I agree with you in that regard, but you have to remember that you cannot question the treatment or dosage prescribed – or *applied* – by highly qualified doctors, Marlene. Just keep your diagnosis to yourself until you retain a stronger position on the food chain here, alright?" the plump sister advised her subordinate.

"Will he be occupying this bed once he leaves the ICU, Sister Barken?" she asked curiously. "Here? With Dr. Gould?"

"Yes. Why not? This is not the Middle Ages or Primary School camp, my dear. We have unisex wards for specific conditions, you know." Sister Barken half-smiled as she reprimanded the star-struck nurse she knew adored Dr. Nina Gould.*Who?* Nina wondered. *Who the hell are they planning to room with me that deserves so much bloody attention?*

"Look, Dr. Gould is frowning," Sister Barken remarked, having no idea it was prompted by Nina's discontent at soon receiving a very unwanted roommate. Silent, waking thoughts were controlling her expression. "It must be the splitting headaches associated with the radiation exposure. Poor thing."*Aye!* Nina thought. *The headaches are killing me, by the way. Your painkillers are a great party favor, but they do jack shit for a throbbing frontal lobe attack, you know?*

Her strong, cold hand suddenly latched onto Nina's wrist, sending a shock through the historian's fever-riddled body that was already sensitive to temperature. Unintentionally, Nina's big, dark eyes shot open.

"Jesus Christ, woman! Do you want to peel my skin off the muscle with that ice-cold talon?" she shrieked. Streaks of pain shot through Nina's nervous system, her thundering response startling both nurses into a stupor.

"Dr. Gould!" Sister Barken exclaimed in surprise in flawless English. "I am so sorry! You are supposed to be under sedation." On the other side of the floor the young nurse grinned from ear to ear.

Realizing that she had just betrayed her charade in the rudest way, Nina elected to play the victim to hide her embarrassment. Immediately she held the side of her head, moaning a little. "Sedation? The pain is coming right through all the painkillers. My apologies for scaring you, but...it – my skin is on fire," Nina performed. Eagerly the other nurse approached her bedside, still smiling like a groupie with a backstage pass.

"Nurse Marx, would you be so kind as to get Dr. Gould something for her headache?" Sister Barken asked. "Bitte," she said a tad louder to jerk young Marlene Marx from her silly fixation.

"Um, yes, of course, Sister," she replied, reluctantly accepting her task before practically skipping out of the room.

"Cute lassie," Nina said.

"Excuse her. She, actually her mother – they are huge fans of yours. They know all about your travels, and some of the things you wrote about quite captivated Nurse Marx. So please ignore her staring," Sister Barken explained amicably.

Nina cut right to the chase while they were unperturbed by the drooling puppy in scrubs that was soon due back. "Who will be sleeping there, then? Anyone I know?"

Sister Barken shook her head. "I don't think he should even know who he is, actually," she whispered. "Professionally I am not at liberty to share, but since you will be sharing a room with the new patient..."

"Guten Morgen, Sister," said a man from the doorway. His words were muffled behind his surgical mask, but Nina could tell that his accent was not authentically German.

"Excuse me, Dr. Gould," said Sister Barken as she walked over to speak to the tall figure. Nina listened attentively. In this sleepy hour it was still relatively quiet in the ward, which made it easier to listen, especially when Nina closed her eyes.

The doctor asked Sister Barken about the young man brought in the night before and why the patient was no longer in what Nina heard as 'Room 4'. Her stomach twitched into a knot when the sister asked for the doctor's credentials and he responded with a threat.

"Sister, if you do not give me the information I need, someone will die before you can call security. Of that I can assure you."

Nina caught her breath. What was he going to do? Even with her eyes wide open she had trouble seeing properly, so attempting to memorize his features was next to futile. It was best just to pretend she could not understand German and that she was too sedated to hear anything anyway.

"No. Do you think it is the first time a charlatan has attempted to intimidate me in my twenty-seven years as a medical professional? Get lost or I will pummel you myself," Sister Barken threatened. The sister said nothing afterward, but Nina distinguished a mad scuffling after which it was alarmingly silent. She dared to turn her head. In the doorway the wall of a woman stood firm, yet the stranger had absconded.

"That was too easy," Nina said under her breath, but played dumb for everyone's sake. "Is that my doctor?"

"No, my dear," Sister Barken replied. "And please, if you see him again, let me or any of the other staff know immediately." She looked very annoyed, but showed no fear whatsoever as she joined Nina at her bed again. "They should bring in the new patient within the next day. They have stabilized him for now. But don't worry, he is under heavy sedation. He will not be a disturbance to you."

"How long will I still be confined here?" Nina asked. "And don't say *until I'm well.*"

Sister Barken chuckled. "You tell me, Dr. Gould. You have everyone amazed at your ability to fight infection and have exhibited borderline supernatural healing capacity. Are you some sort of vampire?"

The nursing sister's humor was most welcome. It cheered Nina to know that there were still individuals with some wonderment. But what she could not relay even to the most open-minded, was that her uncanny ability to heal came from a blood transfusion she had undergone years ago. At the gates of death Nina was saved by the blood of an especially wicked nemesis, an actual remnant of Himmler's experimentations to create a super-human, a wonder weapon. Her name had been *Lita* and she was a monster with powerful blood indeed.

"Maybe the damage was not as profuse as the doctors initially thought," Nina replied. "Besides, if I'm healing so well, why am I going blind?"

Sister Barken caringly laid her hand on Nina's forehead. "Maybe it is just symptomatic of your electrolyte imbalance or your insulin levels, my dear. I am sure your sight will become clearer soon. Don't worry. If you keep going as you are now, you will be out of here soon."

Nina hoped the lady's assumption was right, because she needed to find Sam and ask about Purdue. She needed a new phone as well. Until then, she would just check the news for anything on Purdue, as he was arguably famous enough to make the news in Germany. Even though he had tried to kill her, she hoped he was okay – wherever he was.

"Did the man who brought me in...did he say he would return at all?" Nina inquired about Detlef Holtzer, an acquaintance she had wronged before he rescued her from Purdue and the devil's veins under the infamous Reactor 4 in Chernobyl.

"No, we have not heard from him since," Sister Barken admitted. "Not a boyfriend in any capacity, was he?"

Nina smiled in reminiscence of the sweet, misunderstood bodyguard who had helped her, Sam and Purdue locate the famed Amber Room before things fell apart in the Ukraine. "Not a boyfriend," she smiled at the hazy image of the nursing sister. "A widower."

4

CHARM

"*How* is Nina?" Purdue asked Sam as they vacated the bed-less room with Purdue's coat and a small valise as baggage.

"Detlef Holtzer had her admitted to a hospital in Heidelberg. I am planning to drop in on her in a week or so," Sam whispered as he checked the hallway. "Good thing Detlef is the forgiving type, or else your ass would be haunting Pripyat by now."

Looking first left and right, Sam motioned for his friend to follow him to the right where he was heading for the stairs. They heard voices in discussion coming up to the landing. Hesitating for a moment, Sam stopped and pretended to be embroiled in a conversation on his phone.

"They are not agents of Satan, Sam. Come on," Purdue sniggered, pulling Sam by his sleeve past the two cleaners that were chatting about trivialities. "They don't even know I'm a patient. For all they know, you're *my* patient."

"Mr. Purdue!" a woman called from behind, strategically interrupting Purdue's statement.

"Keep walking," Purdue muttered.

"Why?" Sam teased loudly. "They think I'm your patient, remember?"

"Sam! For God's sake, keep walking," Purdue insisted, only vaguely amused by Sam's juvenile interjection.

"Mr. Purdue, please stop right there. I need to have a word with you," the woman reiterated. He stopped with a sigh of defeat and turned to face the attractive lady. Sam cleared his throat. "Please tell me that is your doctor, Purdue. Because... well, she can brainwash me any day."

"It appears she already has," Purdue mumbled with a sharp look to his associate.

"I have not had the pleasure," she smiled as she met eyes with Sam.

"Would you like to?" Sam asked, receiving a mighty elbow from Purdue.

"Excuse me?" she asked as she joined them.

"He's a bit shy," Purdue lied. "He must learn to speak up, I'm afraid. He must seem so rude, Melissa. I'm sorry."

"Melissa Argyle." She smiled as she introduced herself to Sam.

"Sam Cleave," he said plainly, keeping track of Purdue's surreptitious signals in his peripheral. "Are you Mr. Purdue's..."*Mindfucker?*

"...attending psychologist?" Sam asked, keeping his thoughts locked safely away.

Coyly she scoffed amusedly. "No! Oh, no. I wish I had such authority. I am just the head of administration here at Sinclair, ever since Ella went on maternity leave."

"So you will be leaving in three months?" Sam feigned regret.

"I'm afraid so," she replied. "But it will be okay. I have a free-lance position at Edinburgh University as an assistant, or advisor, to the Dean of Psychology."

"Do you hear that, Purdue?" Sam marveled a bit too much. "She is stationed at Fort Edinburgh! It's a small world. I haunt the place too, but mostly for information when I research my assignments."

"Ah yes," Purdue smiled. "I know where she is – stationed."

"Who do you think got me this position?" she swooned and looked at Purdue with immense adoration. Sam could not let the opportunity for mischief slip by.

"Oh, he did? You old scoundrel, Dave! Helping talented, budding academics into *positions* even when you do not get publicity for it and all. Isn't he just the best, Melissa?" Sam praised his friend, not fooling Purdue at all, but Melissa was convinced of his sincerity.

"I owe Mr. Purdue so much," she chirped. "I just hope he knows how much I appreciate it. As a matter of fact, he gave me this pen." The back of her pen rolled left to right across her dark rose lipstick as she subconsciously flirted, her yellow locks barely covering her hard nipples that strained through her beige cardigan.

"I'm sure that pen appreciates your efforts too," Sam said plainly.

Purdue looked ashen, screaming in his mind for Sam to shut up. The blond woman stopped sucking her pen immediately, realizing what she was doing. "How do you mean, Mr. Cleave?" she asked sternly. Sam was unfazed.

"I mean that pen would appreciate your efforts in signing Mr. Purdue out in a few minutes," Sam smiled confidently. Purdue could not believe it. Sam was busy using his freak talent on Melissa to get her to do what he wished, he realized at once. Trying not to smile at the journalist's audacity, he kept his expression agreeable.

"Absolutely," she beamed. "Just let me pull up the discharge documents and I'll meet you both in the lobby in ten minutes."

"Thank you so much, Melissa," Sam called after her as she descended the stairs.

Slowly his head turned to face Purdue's strange expression.

"You are incorrigible, Sam Cleave," he reprimanded.

Sam shrugged.

"Remind me to buy you a Ferrari for Christmas," he grinned. "But first we're going to drink until Hogmanay and beyond!"

"Rocktober Fest was last week, didn't you know?" Sam said matter-of-factly as the two strolled down to the ground floor reception area.

"Aye."

Behind the reception desk, the flustered girl Sam had bewildered stared at him again. Purdue did not have to ask. He could only guess what mind games Sam must have played on the poor girl. "You know that when you use your powers for evil the gods will take them from you, right?" he asked Sam.

"But I'm not using them for evil. I'm breaking my old pal out of here," Sam defended.

"Not me, Sam. The women," Purdue corrected what Sam already knew was his meaning. "Look at their faces. You did something."

"Nothing they'll regret, sadly. Maybe I should just allow myself a little bit of female attention by means of the gods, hey?" Sam tried to elicit sympathy from Purdue, but he received nothing but a nervous leer.

"Let's just get out of here scot-free first, old boy," he reminded Sam.

"Ha, good choice of words there, sir. Oh look, there is Melissa now," he flashed Purdue a naughty smile. "How *did* she earn that *Caran d'Ache*? With those rosy lips?"

"She belongs to one of my beneficiary programs, Sam, like several other young women...and men, I'll have you know," Purdue defended hopelessly, knowing full well that Sam was pulling his leg.

"Hey, your preferences have nothing to do with me," Sam mocked.

After Melissa signed Purdue's discharge papers, he wasted no time to get to Sam's car on the other side of the enormous botanical garden that surrounded the building. Like two boys playing truant, they walk-jogged away from the facility.

"You have balls, Sam Cleave. I'll give you that," Purdue chuckled as they passed security with the signed release papers.

"I do. Let's prove it though," Sam jested as they got into the car. Purdue's quizzical expression compelled him to give away the secret celebratory venue he had in mind. "Just west of North Berwick we go...to the beer tent village...and we'll be wearing kilts!"

5
___

THE LURKING MARDUK

*W*indowless and dank, the basement lay in quiet wait for the lurking shadow that inked its way along the wall as it slithered down the stairs. Just like a real shadow, the man who cast it moved without a sound as he stole down to the only deserted place he could find to hide long enough until shift change. The emaciated giant plotted his next move meticulously in his mind, but he was in no way oblivious to reality – he would have to lay low for at least another two days.

The latter was a decision made at the scrutiny of the staff roster up on the second floor, where the administrator pinned the week's work schedule to the staff room bulletin board. On the colorful Excel document he'd caught sight of the tenacious nurse's name and her shift details. He did not want to confront her again and she would be on duty for two more days, leaving him no choice other than to squat in the concrete solitude of the slightly illuminated boiler room with only plumbing to amuse him.

What a setback, he thought. But ultimately getting to Flieger

Olaf Löwenhagen, until recently stationed at the Luftwaffe unit at Büchel Air Base, would be worth the wait. The lurking old man could not allow the heavily injured pilot to stay alive at any cost. What the young man could do, should he not be stopped, was simply too risky. The long wait had begun for the deformed hunter, the epitome of patience, now hiding in the depths of the Heidelberg Medical Institution.

In his hands he held the surgical mask he'd just removed, wondering what it would be like to walk among people without some sort of covering over his face. But upon such pondering came the undeniable disdain for the wish. He had to admit to himself that it would vex him immensely to walk in the daylight without a mask, if only for the discomfort it would grant him.

Naked.

He would feel bare, barren as his featureless face was now, if he had to reveal his defect to the world. And he contemplated what it would be like to look normal, by definition, as he sat down in the quiet darkness of the east corner of the basement. Even if he were not plagued by malformation and wore an acceptable face, he would feel exposed and horribly – *visible*. In fact, the only desire he could salvage from the notion was the privilege of proper speech. No, he changed his mind. Being able to speak would not be the only thing that would please him; the joy of smiling itself would be as an elusive dream captured.

He eventually curled up under the coarse cover of a stolen bed linen, courtesy of the laundry room. He'd rolled up a bundle of bloody, tarp-like sheets he'd found in one of the canvas hampers to serve as insulation between his fatless body and the hard floor. After all, his protruding bones bruised his skin even on the mildest of mattresses, but his thyroid did not allow him to gain any of that soft lipid tissue that could gift him comfortable cushioning.

His childhood illness had only exacerbated his birth defect, leaving him a monster in pain. But it was his curse to equalize the blessing of being what he was, he assured himself. At first it had been a hard thing for Peter Marduk to accept, but once he had found his place in the world, his purpose was clear. Handicap, physically or spiritually, would have to give way to his role given by whatever cruel Maker had produced him.

Another day passed and he had gone undetected, his foremost skill in all endeavors. Peter Marduk, aged seventy-eight, laid his head on the stinking linen to get some well-needed sleep while he waited for another day to pass above him. The smell did not bother him. His senses were selective to a fault; one of those blessings he had been cursed with when he hadn't received a nose. When he wanted to track a scent, his sense of smell was like that of a shark. Alternatively, he had the ability to utilize the opposite. That was what he did now.

Switching off his sense of smell, his ears were perked for any normally inaudible disturbance while he was asleep. Blissfully, after more than two full days awake, the old man closed his eyes – his wonderfully normal eyes. Far away, he could hear the squeak of trolley wheels under the weight of Ward B's dinner just before visiting hours. Fading from consciousness rendered him blind and restful, hoping for a dreamless sleep until his task would prompt him to perk up and perform once again.

~

"I AM SO TIRED," Nina told Nurse Marx. The young nurse was on night duty. Since she had become acquainted with Dr. Nina Gould over the past two days, she had slightly abandoned her girl-crush mannerism and adapted a more professional geniality towards the ailing historian.

"Fatigue is part of the illness, Dr. Gould," she told Nina, sympathetically while adjusting her pillows.

"I know, but I haven't felt this tired since I was admitted. Did they give me a sedative?"

"Let me see," Nurse Marx offered. She slid Nina's medical chart from the slot at the foot of her bed and flipped slowly through the pages. Her blue eyes scanned administered drugs of the last twelve hours and then slowly shook her head. "No, Dr. Gould. I see nothing here other than the topical medication in your drip. Certainly no sedatives. Are you feeling sleepy?"

Marlene Marx gently took Nina's arm and checked her vitals. "Your pulse is quite weak. Let me have a look at your BP."

"My God, I feel like I cannot lift my arms, Nurse Marx," Nina sighed heavily. "It feels like..." She had no good way to ask, but in light of the symptoms she was feeling she had to. "Have you ever been *Roofie*'d?"

Looking a little worried that Nina knew what it was like to be under the influence of Rohypnol, the nurse again shook her head. "No, but I have a good idea what a drug like that does to the central nervous system. Is that how you feel?"

Nina nodded, now barely able to open her eyes. Nurse Marx was alarmed to see that Nina's blood pressure was extremely low, crashing in a way that totally belied her previous prognosis. "My body feels like an anvil, Marlene," Nina slurred softly.

"Hang on, Dr. Gould," the nurse said urgently, keeping her voice sharp and loud to wake Nina's mind while she ran to summon her colleagues. Among them was Dr. Eduard Fritz, the physician who had treated the young man who had come in two nights go with the second-degree burns.

"Dr. Fritz!" Nurse Marx called in a tone that would not alarm the other patients, but would relay a level of urgency to the medical staff. "Dr. Gould's BP is dropping rapidly and I'm struggling to keep her conscious!"

The team hastened to Nina's side and pulled the curtains. Onlookers stood stunned at the response of the staff to the small woman who singly occupied the double room. Visiting hours had not seen such action in a long while and a lot of visitors and patients waited to see if the patient would be alright.

"It's like something out of *Grey's Anatomy*," Nurse Marx heard a visitor tell her husband as she ran past with the meds Dr. Fritz had asked for. But all Marx cared about was getting Dr. Gould back before she crashed completely. They opened the curtains again twenty minutes later, conversing in smiling whispers. From the looks on their faces the bystanders knew the patient had been stabilized and returned to the bustling atmosphere usually associated with this time of night at the hospital.

"Thank God we managed to save her," Nurse Marx exhaled

as she leaned on the reception desk to sip a cup of coffee. Little by little visitors started to vacate the ward, saying goodbye to their confined loved ones until the morrow. Gradually the hallways grew quieter as footsteps and subdued tones died down into nothingness. It was a relief to most of the staff members to catch a quick breather before the final rounds of the night.

"Well done, Nurse Marx," Dr. Fritz smiled. It was rare for the man to smile, even at the best of times. As a result, she knew that his words would have to be savored.

"Thank you, Doctor," she replied modestly.

"Really, had you not reacted immediately we may have lost Dr. Gould tonight. I'm afraid her condition is more serious than her biology indicates. I must confess to being confounded by it. You say that her vision had been impaired?"

"Yes, Doctor. She had been complaining that her vision was blurry until last night when she used the words 'going blind' outright. But I was in no position to give her any advise, as I don't have a clue what could be causing it, other than the obvious immune deficiency," Nurse Marx speculated.

"That is what I like about you, Marlene," he said. He was not smiling, but his statement was respectful nonetheless. "You know your place. You do not pretend to be a doctor or presume to tell patients what you think is plaguing them. You leave it to the professionals and that is good. You will go far under my supervision with that attitude."

Hoping that Dr. Hilt did not relay her previous behavior, Marlene only smiled, but her heart went wild with pride at Dr. Fritz's approval. He was one of the foremost authorities in the field of wide spectrum diagnostics ranging from various medical avenues, yet he remained a modest physician and advisor. Considering his career achievements, Dr. Fritz was relatively young. In his late forties, he had already authored several award-winning papers and lectured all over the world during his sabbaticals. His opinion was highly regarded by most medical academics, especially mere nurses like the fresh-from-internship Marlene Marx.

It was true. Marlene knew her place around him. No matter how chauvinist or sexist Dr. Fritz's statement might have sounded, she knew what he meant. However, of the other female staff, there were many who would not have understood his meaning so well. To them, his authority was egotistical, whether he had earned the throne of not. They saw him as a misogynist both in the workplace as well as socially, often speculating about his sexuality. But he paid them no attention. He was only stating the obvious. He knew better and they were not qualified to diagnose out of hand. Therefore, they had no right to give their opinion, least of all when he was on duty to do it properly.

"Look alive, Marx," one of the orderlies said in passing.

"Why? What's happening?" she asked, wide-eyed. She usually prayed for a bit of action during the night shift, but Marlene had had quite enough nervous tension for one night.

"We're moving Freddy Krueger in with the Chernobyl lady," he answered, as he motioned for her to get started on preparing the bed for the transfer.

"Hey, have some bloody respect for the poor man, you

asshole," she told the orderly, who just laughed off her reprimand. "He is someone's son, you know!"

She opened the bed for the new occupant in the faint, lonely light above the bed. Pulling aside the blankets and top sheet to form a neat triangle, if only for the moment, Marlene contemplated the fate of the poor, young man who had lost most of his features, not to mention his abilities from the onslaught of nerve damage. Dr. Gould moved in the shadowy side of the room a few feet away, appearing to be resting well for a change.

They brought in the new patient with a minimum of disruption and transferred him to his new bed, grateful that he was not awake for what would certainly have been unbearable pain during their handling of him. They left quietly once he was settled in, while in the basement slept equally soundly, an imminent menace.

6

DILEMMA IN THE LUFTWAFFE

"My God, Schmidt! I am the commander, the Inspector of the Kommando Luftwaffe!" Harold Meier shrieked in a rare moment of lost control. "These journalists are going to want to know why the missing airman used one of our combat fighters without permission from my office or the Joint Operations Command of the Bundeswehr! And I find out only now that the fuselage has been recovered by our own people – and hidden?"

Gerhard Schmidt, second in command, shrugged and looked at his superior's flushing face. Lieutenant General Harold Meier was not a man to lose control of his emotions. The scene playing before Schmidt was highly unusual, but he understood fully why Meier would react this way. This was a very serious matter, and it would not be long before some snooping journalist got their eye on the truth of the escaped airman, a man who had single-handedly made off with one of their million-Euro planes.

"Has Airman Löwenhagen been found yet?" he asked

Schmidt, the officer unfortunate enough to be designated to bring him the shocking news.

"No. There no body was found at the scene, which leads us to believe that he is still alive," Schmidt responded thoughtfully. "But you must also take into account that he may very well have died in the crash. The explosion could have disintegrated his body, Harold."

"All this 'could have' and 'may have' talk of yours is what bothers me most. The uncertainty of what ensued from the whole affair is what makes me restless, not to mention that some of our squadrons have men on short leave. For the first time in my career I'm feeling anxious," Meier admitted, finally sitting down for a moment to give it some thought. He looked up suddenly, staring into Schmidt's eyes with his own steely gaze, but he was looking further than his subordinate's face. A moment passed before Meier made his eventual decision. "Schmidt..."

"Yes, sir?" Schmidt replied quickly, eager to know how the commander would save them all from embarrassment.

"Take three men you trust. I need sharp men, in brains and brawn, my friend. Men like you. They must understand the trouble we are in. This is a PR nightmare waiting to happen. I – and probably you as well – will most likely be dismissed if what this little shit managed to do under our noses comes out," said Meier, going off on his tangent again.

"And you need us to track him down?" Schmidt asked.

"Yes. And you know what to do if you find him. Use your own discretion. If you wish, interrogate him to find out what madness steered him to this stupid bravery – you know, what his intention was," Meier suggested. He leaned forward with his chin on his folded hands. "But Schmidt, if he even breathes wrong, put him out. We are soldiers after all, not babysitters or psychologists. The collective well being of the Luftwaffe is far more important that one maniacal pissant with something to prove, understand?"

"Completely," Schmidt agreed. He was not just appeasing his superior, but was genuinely of the same mind. The two of them did not come through years of tribulation and training in the German air corps to be undone by some snot nosed airman. As a result, Schmidt was secretly excited about the mission he was being given. He slammed his palms down on his thighs and stood up. "Done. Give me three days to assemble my trio and from there we'll report to you on a daily basis."

Meier nodded, suddenly looking a bit more relieved at the cooperation of a like-minded man. Schmidt replaced his cap and saluted with ceremony, smiling. "That is, if we take that long to resolve this dilemma."

"Let's hope the first report is the last," replied Meier.

"We'll keep in touch," Schmidt promised as he left the office, leaving Meier feeling considerably lighter.

ONCE SCHMIDT HAD CHOSEN his three men, he briefed them under the guise of a covert operation. They must keep knowledge of this mission from all others, including their families and colleagues. In a very tactful manner the officer made sure his men understood that extreme prejudice was the way of the mission. He chose three mild-mannered, intelligent men of differing ranks from different combat units. That was all he needed. He did not bother with details.

"So, gentlemen, do you accept or decline?" he finally asked from atop his makeshift podium, perched on a cement elevation in the on-base repair bay. His stern expression and subsequent silence conveyed the weighty nature of the assignment. "Come on, boys, it's not a marriage proposal! Yes or no! It's a simple mission to find and exterminate a mouse in our wheat silo, boys."

"I'm in."

"Ah, danke Himmelfarb! I knew I chose the right man when I chose you," Schmidt said, bullshitting his way through reverse psychology to push the other two. Thanks to the prevalence of peer pressure, he was eventually successful. Soon after, the red-haired imp called Kohl clicked his heels in his typical ostentatious manner. Naturally the last man, Werner, had to yield. He was reluctant, but only because he had plans to do a bit of gambling in Dillenburg during the next three days and Schmidt's little excursion cock-blocked his plans.

"Let's go get this little prick," he said indifferently. "I beat him twice at Blackjack last month and he owes me 137 Euros anyway."

His two colleagues chuckled. Schmidt was pleased.

"Thank you for volunteering your expertise and time, boys. Let me get my intel tonight and I will have your first orders ready on Tuesday. Dismissed."

7

MEETING THE MURDERER

a cold, black stare of fixed and beady eyes met Nina's as she gradually emerged from her blissful sleep. No nightmares had plagued her this time, yet she'd awoken to this horrid sight nonetheless. She gasped when the dark pupils embedded in bloodshot eyes became a reality she thought she had shed in her slumber.

Oh God, she mouthed at the sight of him.

He responded with what would have been a smile if there had been anything left of his facial muscles, but all she could perceive was the narrowing wrinkle of his eyes in a friendly acknowledgement. He nodded courteously.

"Hello," Nina forced herself to utter, although she was in no mood for conversation. She hated herself for silently hoping the patient had lost his ability for speech, just so she could be left alone. After all, she'd only greeted him in a show of propriety. To her dismay, he answered in a hoarse whisper. "Hello. Sorry I frightened you. It's just that I thought I wouldn't ever wake up again."

Nina smiled without moral coercion this time. "I'm Nina."

"Good to meet you, Nina. I'm sorry...it is difficult to speak," he apologized.

"No worries. Don't speak if it hurts."

"I wish it hurt. But my face is just – numb. It feels..."

He took a deep breath and Nina could see great sorrow in his dark eyes. Suddenly her heart ached for the man with the molten skin, but she dared not speak now. She wanted to let him finish what he wanted to say.

"It feels as though I'm wearing someone else's face." He wrestled with his words, his emotions in turmoil. "Just this dead skin. Just this numbness, like when you touch someone else's face, you know? It feels like – a mask."

As he spoke, Nina imagined his anguish and it made her shun her previous wickedness of wishing him mute for her own comfort. She imagined everything he had told her and put herself in his place. How horrible it must be! But regardless of the reality of his suffering and inevitable handicap, she wanted to keep a positive tone.

"I'm sure it will get better, especially with the drugs they give us," she sighed. "I'm surprised I can feel my ass on the toilet seat."

His eyes narrowed and wrinkled once more, and his gullet expelled a rhythmic gallop that she knew now to be laughter, although the rest of his face showed no sign of it. "Like when you fall asleep on your arm," he added.

Nina pointed at him with a determined concession. "Right on."

Around the two new acquaintances the hospital ward bustled with the morning rounds and delivery of breakfast trays. Nina wondered where Sister Barken was, but said nothing when Dr. Fritz entered the room with two strangers in professional attire and Nurse Marx at their heel. The strangers appeared to be hospital administrators, one male and one female.

"Good morning, Dr. Gould," Dr. Fritz smiled, but he lead his team to the other patient. Nurse Marx gave Nina a quick smile before turning her attention back to her work. They drew the thick green curtains and she heard the staff members chat with the new patient in relatively hushed tones, probably for her sake.

Nina frowned in vexation at their incessant questioning. The poor man could hardly articulate his words properly! Still, she was able to overhear enough to know that the patient could not remember his own name and that the only thing he remembered before he caught fire was flying.

"But you came running in here, still on fire!" Dr. Fritz informed him.

"I don't remember that," the man replied.

Nina closed her failing eyes to heighten her hearing. She heard the doctor say, "My nurse retrieved your wallet when they sedated you. From what we can decipher from the charred remains, you're twenty-seven years old and from Dillenburg. Unfortunately, your name has been destroyed on the card, so we're unable to ascertain who you are or who we should contact about your treatment and such."*Oh my God!* she thought, enraged. *They barely save his life and the*

*first conversation they have with him is about financial triviali-
ties! Typical!*

"I— I have no idea what my name is, doctor. I know even
less about what happened to me." There was a long pause
and Nina could hear nothing until the curtains were parted
again and the two bureaucrats walked out. As they passed,
Nina was appalled to hear one tell the other, "It's not like we
can put an identikit out on the news either. He has no
bloody face to recognize."

She could not resist defending him. "Oi!"

Like good sycophants they stopped and smiled sweetly at
the well-known academic, but what she said wiped the fake
smiles from their faces. "At least that man has one face, not
two. Savvy?"

Without a word the two embarrassed pen pushers left, while
Nina eyed them viciously with one raised eyebrow. Proudly
she pouted, adding softly, "And in flawless German too,
bitches."

"That was impressive German, I must confess, especially for
a Scot." Dr. Fritz was smiling as he wrote in the young man's
file. Both the burn patient and Nurse Marx acknowledged
the feisty historian's chivalry with a thumbs-up that made
Nina feel like her old self again.

NINA SUMMONED NURSE MARX NEARER, making sure the
young woman knew that she wanted to share something
discreet. Dr. Fritz glanced at the two women, suspecting
there was some matter he should be informed of.

"Ladies, I shall be only a moment. Let me just make our patient comfortable." Turning to the burn patient he said, "My friend, we will have to give you a name in the meantime, don't you think?"

"What about *Sam*?" the patient offered.

Nina's stomach tightened up. *I still have to get hold of Sam. Or just Detlef, even.*

"What's the matter, Dr. Gould?" asked Marlene.

"Um, I don't know who else to tell or if this is even pertinent, but," she sighed sincerely, "I think I'm losing my sight!"

"I'm sure it is just a byproduct of the radia...," Marlene tried, but Nina grabbed her arm firmly in protest.

"Listen! If one more member of staff in this hospital uses radiation as an excuse instead of doing something about my eyes, I'm going to start a riot. Do you understand?" She sneered impatiently. "Please. PLEASE. Do something about my eyes. An examination. Anything. I tell you, I'm going blind while Sister Barken assured me I was getting better!"

Dr. Fritz heard Nina's complaint. He tucked his pen in his pocket and left the patient he now called *Sam* with a reassuring wink.

"Dr. Gould, can you see my face or just the outlines of my head?"

"Both, but I cannot detect the color of your eyes, for instance. Everything was blurry before, but now it is becoming impossible to properly see anything further than my arm's reach," Nina replied. "Earlier I could see..." she did not want to call the new patient by his chosen name, but she had to, "...*Sam*'s eyes, even the pinkish color of the whites of his eyes, Doctor. That was literally an hour ago. Now I can't distinguish anything."

"Sister Barken told you the truth," he said as he pulled out his light pen and pried Nina's eyelids apart with a gloved left hand. "You are healing up very quickly, almost unnaturally." He had sunk his almost barren face down next to hers to check the response of her pupils when she gasped.

"I see you!" she cried. "I see you clear as day. Every blemish. Even the stubble on your face that is peeking from the pores."

Perplexed, he looked at the nurse on the other side of Nina's bed. Her face was full of concern. "We'll run some blood tests later today. Nurse Marx, have the results ready for me tomorrow."

"Where is Sister Barken?" Nina asked.

"She is off-duty until Friday, but I'm sure a promising nurse like Ms. Marx here can take care of it, right?" The young nurse nodded zealously.

ONCE THE EVENING visiting hours were over, most of the staff were busy preparing the patients for the night, but Dr. Fritz had had Dr. Nina Gould sedated earlier on to make sure that she slept properly. She had been rather upset all day, behaving unlike her usual self because of her waning eyesight. Uncharacteristically, she had been reserved and a bit morose, as was expected. By lights out she was fast asleep.

By 3:20 a.m. even the subdued chatting between the nurses on the night staff had ceased, and they were all fighting the various attacks of boredom and the lulling power of silence. Nurse Marx was pulling an extra shift, spending her free moments on social media. It was a pity that she was professionally forbidden from posting the admission of her heroine, Dr. Gould. She was sure it would have provoked the envy of the History Majors and World War II fanatics among her online friends, but alas, she had to keep the awesome news to herself.

The light clapping sound of skipping footsteps came up the hallway before Marlene looked up and found one of the orderlies from the First Floor racing toward the nurses' station. An unfit janitor ran in his wake. Both men wore faces of shock, frantically urging the nurses to hush before they reached them.

Out of breath, the two men stopped at the door of the office where Marlene and another nurse waited to receive an explanation for their strange behavior.

"There – th-there is," the janitor started first, "an in-intruder on the Ground Floor and he is coming up the stairs of the fire escape as we speak."

"So, call security," Marlene whispered, surprised at their ineptitude at handling a security risk. "If you suspect that someone is posing a threat to the staff and patients, you know you…"

"Listen, sweetheart!" The orderly leaned up right against the young woman, sneering in her ear as quietly as he could. "Both security officers are dead!"

The janitor nodded wildly. "It's true! Call the police. Now! Before he gets up here!"

"What about the second floor staff?" she asked, frantically trying to find a line from Reception. The two men shrugged. Marlene was dismayed to find that the switchboard tone was beeping incessantly. This meant there were either too many calls to process or a faulty system.

"I cannot get hold of the main lines!" she whispered urgently. "Oh my God! Nobody knows there is trouble. We have to warn them!" Marlene used her cell phone to call Dr. Hilt on his private cell phone. "Dr. Hilt?" she said wide-eyed while the anxious men constantly checked for the shape they had seen going up the fire stairs.

"He is going to be pissed that you called him on his cell phone," the orderly warned.

"Who gives a shit? As long as she gets a hold of him, Victor!" the other nurse grunted. She followed suit, using her cell phone to call the local police while Marlene tried Dr. Hilt's number again.

"He's not answering," she panted. "It rings, but there is no voicemail either."

"Great! And our phones are in our fucking lockers!" the orderly, Victor, fumed hopelessly, running his frustrated fingers through his hair. In the background they heard the other nurse speak to the police. She shoved her phone against the orderly's chest.

"Here!" she urged. "Tell them the details. They're sending two cars."

Victor explained the situation to the emergency operator, who dispatched the patrol vehicles. He then stayed on the line while she continued to obtain more information from him and conveyed it over the radio to the patrol cars as they rushed to the Heidelberg Hospital.

8

IT'S ALL FUN AND GAMES UNTIL...

"*M*ake zigzags! I need a challenge!" the rowdy, overweight woman roared as Sam started bolting away from the table. Purdue was too drunk to be alarmed as he watched Sam try to win his wager that the heavy-set, knife-wielding lass could not hit him. The nearest drinkers around them had formed a small mob of cheering and betting hooligans, all familiar with Big Moragh's talent with blades. They all lamented, and wished to profit from, the misguided courage of this idiot from Edinburgh.

Tents were alight with festivities in lantern glow, casting shadows of swaying drunkards singing heartily along with the folk band's pipes. It was not quite dark yet, but the heavy, overcast sky reflected the fires from the wide field below. On the snaking river that ran along the stalls, some people were on rowboats, enjoying the quiet ripples of the glimmering water around them. Under the fringe of trees near the parking area, children were playing.

Sam heard the first dagger swoosh past his shoulder.

52

"Ai!" he yelled inadvertently. "Almost spilled my ale there!"

He heard the screaming women and men egging him on through the din of Moragh's fans chanting her name. Somewhere in the madness, Sam heard a small group chanting *"Knife the bampot! Knife the bampot!"*

From Purdue there was no support, even when Sam turned around briefly to see where Moragh had shifted her aim. Wearing his family's tartan on his kilt, Purdue was staggering through the mad lot in the direction of the clubhouse on the site.

"Traitor," Sam slurred. He took another chug of his ale just as Moragh lifted her flabby arm to line the last of the three daggers. "Oh shit!" Sam exclaimed and tossed aside his tankard to make a run for the hillock by the river.

As he had dreaded, his inebriation served two purposes – delivery of humiliation and then the subsequent aptitude not to give a rat's ass. His disorientation on the turn caused him to abandon his equilibrium and after only one leap forward his foot slapped the back of his other ankle, bringing him down onto the wet, loose grass and mud with a thump. Sam's skull struck a rock buried in the long tufts of greenery and a bright flash pumped through his brain painfully. His eyes rolled back in their sockets, but he regained his consciousness instantaneously.

The velocity of his tumble sent his heavy kilt lashing forward when his body stopped short. On his lower back he could feel the awful confirmation of the upturned raiment. If that was not affirmation enough of the ensuing nightmare, the crisp air on his buttocks did the trick.

"Oh Christ! Not again," he moaned through the smell of

mud and manure as the roaring laughter of the crowd punished him. "On the upside," he said to himself as he sat up, "in the morning I won't remember this. That's right! It won't matter."

But he was a terrible journalist for neglecting to remember that the flashing lights sporadically blinding him from a short distance away meant that even while he would forget the ordeal, pictures would prevail. For a moment Sam just sat there, wishing he had not been as painfully traditional; wishing he had worn briefs, or at least a thong! Moragh's toothless mouth was wide open in laughter as she wobbled closer to collect him.

"Dun't ya worreh, sweeteh!" she chuckled. "Those'r nee the werst eyv seen!"

With one swift movement the stout lass pulled him to his feet. Sam was too drunk and nauseous to fight her off as she dusted his kilt off and copped a feel while she helped herself to a bit of comedy at his expense.

"Oi! Eh, lady..." he blundered his words. His arms flailed like a drugged flamingo as he tried to recover his composure. "Watch yer hands there!"

"Sam! Sam!" he heard from somewhere inside the bubble of cruel mocking and whistling coming from the big grey tent.

"Purdue?" he called, searching the thick muddy lawn for his tankard.

"Sam! Come, we have to go! Sam! Stop playing around with the fat woman!" Purdue staggered along, slurring as he neared.

"What ye seh?" Moragh shouted at the insult. Scowling, she left Sam's side to give Purdue her full attention.

"SOME ICE ON THAT, MATE?" the bartender asked Purdue.

Sam and Purdue had entered the clubhouse on wavering legs after most of the people had already vacated their seats, opting to go outside and see the flame eaters during the drum show.

"Aye! Ice for both of us," Sam cried, holding the side of his head where the stone had connected. Purdue swaggered by his side, arm held aloft to order two meads while they nursed their injuries.

"My God, that woman hits like Mike Tyson," Purdue remarked, as he pressed the ice pack against his right brow, the place where Moragh's first shot had marked her discontent at his uttering. Her second had landed just short of his left cheekbone, and Purdue could not help but be just a tad impressed at her combination.

"Well, she throws knives like an amateur," Sam chipped in, as he clenched the glass in his hand.

"You do know that she did not really aim to hit you, right?" the barman reminded Sam. He gave it some thought and retorted, "But then, she is daft to make such a wager. I won double my money back."

"Aye, but she bet against herself at four times the odds, laddie!" the barman cackled heartily. "She didn't get this reputation by being stupid, eh?"

"Ha!" Purdue exclaimed, his eyes glued to the TV screen

behind the bar. It was the very reason he had come looking for Sam in the first place. Something he saw on the news earlier had struck him as reason for concern, and he wanted to sit there until the bulletin repeated so he could show Sam.

On the next hour the screen displayed exactly what he had been waiting for. He edged forward, knocking over some glasses on the counter. "Look!" he exclaimed. "Look, Sam! Isn't that the hospital where our dear Nina is at the moment?"

Sam watched the reporter talk about the drama that had hit the well-known hospital just hours before. It alarmed him instantly. The two men exchanged looks of concern.

"We have to go and get her, Sam," Purdue insisted.

"If I were sober I would go right now, but we can't travel to Germany in this state," Sam lamented.

"That's not a problem, my friend," Purdue smiled in his usual mischievous way. He lifted his glass and emptied the last bit of alcohol from it. "I have a private jet and a crew who can fly us there while we sleep it off. Much as I'm reluctant to fly to Detlef's neck of the woods again, this is Nina we are speaking of."

"Aye," Sam agreed. "I don't want her staying there one more night. Not if I can help it."

Purdue and Sam left the festivities, thoroughly shitfaced and somewhat knackered by cuts and scratches, determined to get their heads cleared and come to the aid of the other third of their social alliance.

As the night fell over the Scottish coast they left in their trail the jovial abandon, listening to the bagpipes fade. It was a harbinger of more serious things, where their momentary recklessness and fun would have to give way to the urgent rescue of Dr. Nina Gould, who was sharing space with a loose killer.

9

CRY OF THE FACELESS

*N*ina was terrified. She'd slept through most of the morning and early afternoon, but Dr. Fritz had her taken to the examination room for her eye tests as soon as the police had allowed them to move around. The ground floor was being heavily guarded both by police as well as the on-site security company who had sacrificed two of their men during the night. The second floor was off-limits for anyone not confined there, or the medical staff.

"You're fortunate you were able to sleep through all the madness, Dr. Gould," Nurse Marx told Nina as she came to check on her in the evening.

"I don't even know what happened, really. There were security men killed by an intruder?" Nina frowned. "That's what I was able to make out by the drips and drabs of what was discussed. Nobody could tell me what the hell is really going on."

Marlene looked around to make sure nobody saw her telling Nina the details.

"We're not supposed to alarm the patients with too much information, Dr. Gould," she said under her breath, pretending to check Nina's vitals. "But last night, one of our janitors saw someone kill one of the security men. Of course, he did not stick around to see who it was."

"Did they catch the intruder?" Nina asked seriously.

The nurse shook her head. "That is why the place is in lock-down. They are searching the hospital for anyone who isn'tt authorized to be here, but so far no luck."

"How is that possible? He must have slipped out before the cops came," Nina speculated.

"That's what we think too. I just don't understand what he was looking for that was worth the lives of two men," Marlene said. She gave a deep sigh and decided to change the subject. "How is your sight today? Better?"

"Same," Nina replied indifferently. Clearly other things were on her mind.

"With the interference now, it will take a bit longer to get your results. But as soon as we know, we can start treatment."

"I hate feeling like this. I'm drowsy all the time and now I can hardly see more than a fuzzy rendition of the people I encounter," Nina moaned. "You know, I need to get in touch with my friends and family so that they will know I'm okay. I cannot stay here forever."

"I understand, Dr. Gould," Marlene sympathized, glancing back at her other patient opposite Nina who was stirring in his bed. "Let me go check on Sam over there."

As Nurse Marx approached the burn victim, Nina watched him open his eyes and look at the ceiling as if he could see something they could not. Then a sorrowful nostalgia came over her and she whispered to herself.

"Sam."

Nina's fading sight catered to her curiosity as she watched *Sam the patient* lift his hand and clutch Nurse Marx's wrist, but she could not discern the expression on his face. Nina's own reddened skin, damaged by the toxic air of Chernobyl, was virtually completely healed. But still she felt as if she were dying. Nausea and dizziness prevailed, while her vitals showed only improvement. For someone as adventurous and fiery as the Scottish historian, such perceived weaknesses were unacceptable and dealt her a considerable amount of frustration.

She could hear whispering before Nurse Marx shook her head, negating whatever he had requested. The nurse pulled free of the patient and briskly left without looking at Nina. The patient, however, was looking at Nina. That much she could see. But she had no idea why. Characteristically, she confronted him.

"What is it, Sam?"

He did not look away, yet he remained quiet, as if he hoped she would forget that she had addressed him. Trying to sit up, he groaned in pain and fell back on his pillow again. He sighed wearily. Nina decided to leave him be, but then his hoarse words broke the silence between them, demanding her attention.

"Y-you know...know...the man they're looking for?" he stammered. "You know? The intruder?"

"Aye," she replied.

"He is after m-me. It's me he is looking for, Nina. A-and tonight...he is coming to kill me," he said in a quivering mumble of mispronounced words. It ran Nina's blood cold, what he said, because she had not expected the culprit to be searching for anything in her vicinity. "Nina?" he urged for a response.

"Are you sure?" she asked.

"I am," he affirmed, to her dread.

"Look, how do you know who it is? Did you see him here? Did you see him with your own eyes? Because if you didn't, chances are you're just being paranoid, my friend," she stated, hoping to help him think over his assessment to bring him some clarity. She also hoped that he was mistaken, as she was in no condition to be evading a killer. She saw his wheels turn as he considered her words. "Another thing," she added, "if you cannot even remember who you are or what happened to you, how do you know that some faceless assailant is after you?"

Nina was not aware of it, but her choice of words reversed all of the effects the young man was suffering from – memories now flooded back in. His eyes grew wide in terror as she spoke, piercing her with their black gaze so strongly that she could see it even through her dwindling sight.

"Sam?" she asked. "What is it?"

"Mein Gott, Nina!" he wheezed. It was actually a scream, but the damage to his voice box smothered it into a mere hysterical whisper. "Faceless, you say! F-face-faceless! He was... Nina, the man who set me on fire...!"

"Aye? What about him?" she pushed, although she knew what he was revealing. She just wanted more details, if she could get them.

"The man who tried to kill me...h-he had...no face!" the horrified patient wailed. If he could cry, he would have sobbed at the memory of the monstrous man who'd pursued him after the game that night. "He caught up with me and he set me on fire!"

"Nurse!" Nina hollered. "Nurse! Somebody! Please help!"

Two nurses came running with quizzical expressions. Nina pointed to the upset patient and exclaimed, "He just remembered his attack. Please give him something for the shock!"

They raced to his aid and pulled the curtains, administering a sedative to calm him. Nina felt her own lethargy threaten, but she tried to unravel the strange puzzle by herself. Was he serious? Was he coherent enough to make such an accurate call or was he making it up? She doubted that he was insincere. After all, the man could hardly move on his own or utter a sentence without struggle. He certainly would not be so frantic if he were not convinced that his incapacitated state would cost him his life.

"God, I wish Sam was here to help me think," she murmured as her mind begged to sleep. "Even Purdue would do, if he could refrain from trying to kill me this time." It was coming on dinner time already and, since neither of them expected visitors, Nina was free to sleep if she wished. Or so she thought.

Dr. Fritz smiled as he walked in. "Dr. Gould, I'm just coming to give you something for the eye problem."

"Shit," she muttered. "Hello doctor. What are you giving me?"

"Just a treatment to alleviate the tightening of the capillaries in your eyes. I have reason to believe that your sight is being impaired by constricted circulation in your ocular area. If you have any trouble throughout the night you can just call on Dr. Hilt. He'll be on duty again tonight and I'll check in with you in the morning, okay?"

"Alright, doctor," she agreed, watching him inject the unknown substance into her arm. "Do you have the test results yet?"

Dr. Fritz pretended not to hear her at first, but Nina repeated her question. He did not look up at her, apparently concentrating on what he was doing. "We'll discuss that tomorrow, Dr. Gould. I should have the lab results back by then." He finally looked up at her with failed reassurance, but she was in no mood to pursue the matter any further. By now her roommate had calmed down and grown silent. "Good night, dear Nina." He smiled kindly and pressed Nina's hand before closing her file and replacing it at the foot of her bed.

"Good night," she hummed, as the drug took course and lulled her mind away.

10

ESCAPE FROM SAFETY

a boney finger poked Nina's arm, starting her into a frightful awakening. Reflexively she clamped her hand down onto the touched area, unexpectedly catching a hand under her palm that scared her half to death. Her inadequate eyes sprang wide open to see what was accosting her, but apart from the piercing dark spots under the brow of the plastic mask, she could not discern the face.

"Nina! Shh," the empty face implored in a soft rasp. It was her roommate, standing by her bed in his white hospital gown. The tubes had been removed from his arms, leaving trails of oozing crimson wiped away carelessly on the barren white skin around it.

"W-what the hell?" she frowned. "Seriously?"

"Listen, Nina. Just keep very quiet and listen to me," he whispered, sinking to his haunches a little so that his body was obscured from the entrance of the room by Nina's bed. Only his head was elevated above so that he could speak in her ear. "The man I told you about is going to come looking for me. I have to find a hiding place until he is gone."

But he was out of luck. Nina was drugged into delirium and did not care much for his fate. She just nodded until her free floating eyes disappeared under the cover of heavy lids again. He sighed in despair and looked around, his breath increasing with every passing moment. Yes, there was the police presence protecting the patients, but honestly, armed protection hadn't even saved the men who were employed by it, let alone those who were unarmed!

It would be best, *Sam the patient* thought, if he hid instead of risking an escape. If he were to be discovered, he could then deal with the assailant accordingly and hopefully Dr. Gould would not be harmed by any ensuing violence. Nina's ears had improved vastly since she had begun losing her sight; this allowed her to she stayed tuned-in to the shuffling feet of her paranoid roommate. One after the other, his footsteps withered away from her, but not towards his bed. She kept drifting in and out of sleep, but her eyes remained shut.

Soon after, deep behind Nina's ocular cavities a numbing pain had blossomed, bleeding out in a flower of hurt through her brain. Nerve connections quickly introduced her receptors to the splitting migraine it was causing, and Nina yelped out loud in her sleep. Suddenly, the gradually growing headache filled her eyeballs and set her brow on fire with fever.

"Oh my God!" she shouted. "My head! My head is killing me!"

Her cries echoed through the practical silence of the dead of night in the ward, promptly summoning the medical staff to her side. Nina's shivering thumbs finally fumbled their way to the emergency button and she pressed it repeatedly to illicit help from the night nurse. A new nurse, fresh from the academy, came rushing in.

"Dr. Gould? Dr. Gould, are you alright? What is the matter, dear?" she asked.

"M-my...," Nina stuttered through her drug-induced disorientation, "head is exploding with pain! It sits right behind my eyes now and it is killing me. My God! It feels as if my skull is cracking open."

"I'll go and get Dr. Hilt quickly. He just came out of surgery. Just relax. He'll be by just now, Dr. Gould." The nurse turned and hastened out for help.

"Thank you," Nina sighed, exhausted from the hideous pain, no doubt courtesy of her eyes. Briefly, she lifted her head to check on *Sam the patient*'s , but he was absent. Nina frowned. *I could have sworn he spoke to me while I was sleeping.* She thought about it further. *No. I must have been dreaming.*

"Dr. Gould?"

"Aye? Sorry, I can hardly see," she apologized.

"Dr. Hilt is with me." Turning to the doctor she said, "Excuse me, I just have to run next door for a moment to help Frau Mittag with her bed pan."

"Of course, Nurse. Please take your time," the doctor replied. Nina heard the nurse's feet patter out lightly. She looked at Dr. Hilt and informed him of her exact complaint. Unlike Dr. Fritz, who was very active and liked to diagnose swiftly, Dr. Hilt was a better listener. He waited for Nina to explain

66

precisely how the headache settled behind her eyes before responding.

"Dr. Gould? Can you at least see me properly?" he asked. "The headaches usually are directly connoted with the impending blindness, you see?"

"Not at all," she said morosely. "This blindness seems to be getting worse every day and Dr. Fritz has not done anything constructive about it. Can you please just give me something for the pain? It's almost unbearable."

He removed his surgical mask to speak clearly. "Of course, my dear."

She saw him tilt his head, looking over to Sam's bed. "Where is the other patient?"

"I don't know," she shrugged. "Maybe he went to the toilet. I remember he told Nurse Marx that he had no intention of using a bed pan."

"Why would he not use the toilet here?" the doctor asked, but Nina was quite frankly becoming really sick of reporting on her roommate when she needed help to alleviate her splitting headache.

"I don't know!" she snapped at him. "Look, can you please just give me something for the pain?"

He was not impressed with her tone at all, but inhaled deeply and sighed. "Dr. Gould, are you hiding your roommate?"

The question was both absurd and unprofessional. Utter annoyance coursed through Nina at his ridiculous question. "Aye. He is somewhere in the room. Twenty points if you can give me a painkiller before you find him!"

"You have to tell me where he is, Dr. Gould, or you will die tonight," he said plainly.

"Are you absolutely daft?" she shrieked. "Are you seriously threatening me?" Nina felt that something was very wrong, but she could not cry out. With blinking eyes she watched him, her fingers furtively seeking the red button that was still on her bed next to her while she kept her eyes on his missing face. His blurry shadow lifted the call button for her to discern. "Are you looking for this?"

"Oh Christ," Nina wept at once, burying her nose and mouth behind her palms as she realized that she recalled that voice now. Her head was pounding and her skin burning wet, but she dared not move.

"Where is he?" he whispered evenly. "Tell me, or you will die."

"I don't know, alright?" her voice quivered softly behind her hands. "I really don't know. I've been sleeping all this time. My God, am I his keeper?"

The tall man replied, "You are quoting Cain, straight out of the Bible. Tell me, Dr. Gould, are you religious?"

"Fuck you!" she yelled.

"Ah, an Atheist," he remarked speculatively. "*There are no atheists in fox holes.* That is another quote – perhaps one more suited for you in this moment of final restitution, where you will meet your death at the hands of something you will wish you had a god for."

"You are not Dr. Hilt," the nurse said behind him. Her words came like a question dipped in disbelief and realization. Then he struck her down with such elegant speed that Nina did not even have time to register the brevity of his act. As the nurse fell, her hands released the bedpan. It went sliding along the polished floor in a deafening clatter that immediately drew the attention of night staff at the nurses' station.

From nowhere, police officers started shouting down the hall. Nina waited for them to seize the imposter in her room, but instead they darted right past her door.

"Go! Go! Go! He is on the Second Floor! Corner him in the Dispensary! Quick!" the commanding officer was shouting.

"What?" Nina scowled. She could not believe it. All she could distinguish was the figure of the charlatan rapidly moving towards her and, just like the fate of the poor nurse, he landed a mighty blow on her head. She felt immense pain for a moment before dissolving into the black river of oblivion.Nina came to only moments later, still uncomfortably contorted on her bed. Her headache now had company. The blow on her temple taught her a new level of pain. It was now swollen so that her right eye felt smaller. On the floor beside her, the night nurse was still lying sprawled, but Nina had no time. She had to get out before the eerie stranger made his way back to her, especially now that he knew her better.

She grabbed for the dangling call button again, but the head of the device had been severed. "Shit," she moaned, carefully swinging her legs off the side of the bed. All she could see were the mere outlines of objects and people. There was no indication of identity or intent when she could not see their faces.

"Fuck! Where are Sam and Purdue when I need them? How do I always end up in this shit?" she whined half between vexation and fear as she went, feeling her way to relieving herself of the tubes in her arms and navigating past the heap of woman next to her uncertain feet. The police action had drawn the attention of most night staff and Nina noticed that the Third Floor was eerily quiet, save for the distant echo of a television weather report and two patients whispering in the next room.*Clear*. It prompted her to find her clothing and get dressed as best as she could in the gaining darkness of her diminishing vision that would soon abandon her. After she was dressed, her boots in her hands to avert arousing suspicion when she walked out, she snuck back to Sam's bedside table and opened his drawer. His charred wallet was still inside. She removed the license card inside, slipping it into the back pocket of her jeans.

She was beginning to worry about her roommate's where-abouts, his condition, and most of all – if his desperate petitioning had not perhaps been real. Thus far she had only considered it a dream, but with him missing she was starting to think twice about his visit earlier that night. Either way, she now had to escape the impostor. The police could offer no protection against a threat with no face. Already they had ran after suspects without any one of them having actually seen the man responsible. The only way Nina knew who was responsible was by his reprehensible manner with her and Sister Barken.

"Oh shit!" she said, stopping in her tracks, almost at the end of the white hallway. "Sister Barken. I have to warn her." But

Nina knew that asking for the stout nursing sister would alert staff that she was sneaking out. There was no doubt they would not allow that. *Think, think, think!* Nina urged herself as she stood still, wavering. She knew what she had to do. It was unsavory, but it was the only way.

Back in her dark room, using only the hallway light shining in on the glimmering floor, Nina began undressing the night nurse. Fortunately for the small historian, the nurse was two sizes larger than she was.

"I'm so sorry. Really, I am," Nina whispered as she stripped the woman of her scrubs and put them on over her clothing. Feeling rather awful for what she was doing to the poor woman, Nina's clumsy morality drove her to drape her bedclothes over the nurse. After all, the lady was in her underwear on a cold floor. *Give her a roll there, Nina,* she thought on a second look. *No, that's stupid. Just get the fuck out of here!* But the nurse's motionless body seemed to call to her. Perhaps it was the blood that came from her nose, blood that had formed a sticky, dark puddle on the floor under her face, that provoked Nina's pity. *We don't have time!* the forceful reasoning reprimanded her pondering. "Fuck it," Nina decided out loud, and gave the unconscious lady a roll over once so that the bedding would wrap her body and keep her insulated from the hardness of the floor.

As a nurse, Nina would be able to foil police officers and get out, as long as they did not notice that she was having trouble finding steps and doorknobs. When she finally made it down to the Ground Floor, she overheard two officers talking about the murder victim.

"Wish I was here," one said. "I'd have caught that son of a bitch."

"Of course all the action happens *before* our shift. Now we're stuck babysitting what's left," the other bemoaned.

"This time the victim was a doctor – on night duty," the first one whispered. *Dr. Hilt, perhaps?* she thought as she headed for the exit.

"They discovered this doctor with a piece of his facial skin peeled off, just like the one security guard of the night before," she heard him add.

"Shift over early?" one of the officers asked Nina as she passed. She caught her breath and formulated her German as best she could.

"Yes, my nerves did not handle the murder well. Passed out and hit my face," she replied in a quick mumble as she tried to find the door handle.

"Let me get that for you," someone said, and opened the door amidst their expressions of sympathy.

"Have a good night, nurse," the police officer told Nina.

"Danke schön," she smiled as she felt the cool night air on her face, fighting her headache and trying not to tumble over the steps.

"And you have a good night too, doctor...*Hilt*, is it?" the cop asked behind Nina at the door. Her blood froze in her veins, but she kept true.

"That is correct. Good night, gentlemen," the man said cheerfully. "Stay safe!"

11

MARGARET'S CUB

"*S*am Cleave is the just the man for this, sir. I'll get in touch with him."

"We cannot afford Sam Cleave," Duncan Gradwell answered quickly. He was dying for a cigarette, but when the news of the fighter plane crash in Germany came over the wire on his computer screen, it demanded instant and urgent attention.

"He is an old friend of mine. I'll...twist his arm," he heard Margaret. "Like I said, I'll get in touch with him. We worked together years ago when I assisted his fiancée, Patricia, with her first piece as a professional."

"Is that the girl who was shot dead in front of him by that arms ring whose operation they busted open?" Gradwell asked in a rather insensitive way. Margaret sank her head and replied with a slow nod. "No wonder he took to the bottle so strongly in the years after that," Gradwell sighed.

Margaret had to chuckle at that. "Well, sir, Sam Cleave did

not need much coaxing to suck on a bottle neck. Not before Patricia, nor after the – *incident*."

"Ah! So tell me, is he too unstable to cover this story for us?" Gradwell asked.

"Aye, Mr. Gradwell. Sam Cleave is not only reckless, he's infamous for a bit of a bent mind," she said with a fond smile. "Which is precisely the caliber of journalist you want to blow open the covert operations of the command of the German Luftwaffe. I'm sure their Chancellor will be thrilled to know about it, especially now."

"I agree," Margaret affirmed, locking her hands in front of her while she stood at attention in front of her editor's desk. "I will get hold of him immediately and see if he'll be willing to knock some off his fee for an old friend."

"I should hope so!" Gradwell's double chin shivered as his voice escalated. "The man is a celebrated author now, so I am sure these insane excursions he embarks on with that rich idiot are not a feat of necessity."

The 'rich idiot' Gradwell so fondly referred to was David Purdue. Gradwell had cultivated an increasing disrespect for Purdue through the recent years, due to the billionaire's snubbing of a personal friend of Gradwell's. The friend in question, Professor Frank Matlock of Edinburgh University, had been forced to resign as Department Head in the much clamored over Brixton Tower after Purdue had ceased his generous endowments towards the department. Naturally, a furor ensued over Purdue's subsequent romantic involvement with Matlock's favorite chew toy, the object of his misogynistic by-laws and reservations, Dr. Nina Gould.

The fact that this was all ancient history worthy of a decade and a half of water under the bridge made no difference to a bitter Gradwell. Now he was running the Edinburgh Post, a position he had attained with hard work and fair play, years after Sam Cleave had deserted the dusty halls of the newspaper.

"Yes, Mr. Gradwell," Margaret replied politely. "I'll get a hold of him, but what if I'm not successful in reeling him in?"

"In two weeks of world history will be made, Margaret," Gradwell smirked like a Halloween rapist. "In just over a week the world will watch a live broadcast from the Hague, where the Middle East and Europe will sign a peace treaty to ensure the cessation of all military hostilities between the two worlds. A sure threat to that happening is the recent suicide flight of Dutch pilot Ben Grijsman, remember?"

"Yes, sir." She bit her lip, knowing full well where he was going with this, but refusing to provoke his wrath by interrupting. "He got into an Iraqi air base and stole a plane."

"That's right! And crashed into the C.I.T.E. Head Quarters creating the fuck-up now unfolding. As you know, the Middle East obviously sent someone to retaliate by rogering a German air base!" he exclaimed. "Now tell me again how the reckless and sharp Sam Cleave will *not* jump at the chance to get into this story."

"Point taken," she smiled coyly, feeling deeply uncomfortable at having to watch her boss produce threads of saliva while he spoke passionately about the nascent situation. "I should go. Who knows where he is these days? I'll have to start calling around promptly."

"That's right!" Gradwell roared after her as she made a beeline for her small office. "Hurry and get Cleave to cover this for us before another anti-peace prick gets a boner for suicide and brings about World War III!"

Margaret did not even glance at her colleagues as she rushed past them, but she knew that they were all having a good laugh at the delightful phrases Duncan Gradwell spat out. His choice words were an office joke. Margaret usually laughed loudest when the veteran editor of six prior press offices started getting excited about the news, but now she did not dare. What if he saw her giggle at what he considered to be a seriously newsworthy assignment? Imagine what he would thunder if he saw her smirk reflected in the large glass panels of her office?

Margaret looked forward to speaking to young Sam again. Then again, he had not been *young* Sam for a while now. But to her, he would always be the wayward and over-zealous news snout out to expose injustice wherever he could. He had been Margaret's understudy in the previous era of the *Edinburgh Post,* when the world was still in the chaos of liberalism and the conservatives wanted to tighten the very freedom of every individual. Things had swung around drastically since the World Unity Organization took over the political administration of several former EU countries and several South American territories had broken away from what had once been Third World governments.

Margaret was not a feminist by any reach, but the World Unity Organization being predominantly run by women had showed a considerable difference in how they governed and resolved political tension. War efforts no longer enjoyed the favor they'd once received from male-dominated governments. Now, achievements in problem solving, invention and the optimization of resources profited from international endowments and investment strategies.

At the head of the W.U.O. was the chair of what was instituted as the Council for International Tolerance Efforts, Professor Marta Sloane. She was a former Polish ambassador to England who had won the last election to run the new union of nations. The Council's main objective was to eliminate war threats by engaging in treaties of mutual compromise instead of terrorism and military engagement. Trade was more important than political hostility, Prof. Sloane always imparted in her speeches. In fact, it became a principle associated with her in all media.

"Why do we have to lose our sons in their thousands to sate the greed of a handful of old men sitting in office where war will never affect them?" she was heard proclaiming only days before she was elected by a landslide victory. "Why do we have to cripple economies and destroy the hard work of architects and masons? Or destroy buildings and kill innocent people, while modern warlords profit from our heartbreak and the severing of our bloodlines? Youth sacrificed to serve the unending circle of destruction is madness, perpetuated by the feeble-minded leaders presiding over your future. Parents losing their children, spouses lost, brothers and sisters ripped from us because of the ineptitude of aged and bitter men at resolving conflict?"

With her dark hair taken back in a braid and her trademark velvet choker that matched whatever suit she wore, the petite, charismatic leader shook the world with her seemingly simple cures for the destructive practices practiced by religious and political systems. In fact, once she'd been ridiculed by her official opposition for claiming that the spirit of the Olympics had turned into nothing but another exuberant fiscal generator.

She insisted that it should have been employed for the same reasons it was begotten – peaceful competition by which the winner is determined without casualties. "Why can we not go to war on a chess board, or on a tennis court? Even an arm wrestling match between two countries could determine which gets their way, for goodness sake! It's the very same idea, only without the billions spent on military material or the countless lives destroyed by casualties between foot soldiers who have nothing to do with the proximal cause. These people kill each other, having no reason other than orders to do so! If you, my friends, cannot walk up to someone in the street and shoot them in the head without regret or psychological trauma," she asked from her podium in the city of Minsk a while ago, "why do you force your children and siblings and spouses to do it by voting for these old-fashioned tyrants that perpetuate this atrocity? Why?"

Margaret did not care if the new unions were criticized for what the opposition campaigns called *the advent of feminist rule* or *the insidious coup by agents of the Anti-Christ*. She would support any ruler who stood against the senseless mass murder of our own human race in the name of power, greed and corruption. In essence, Margaret Crosby supported Sloane because the world was less heavy since she'd come to power. Dark veils that had covered age-old feuds were now addressed outright, allowing a channel of communication between begrudged countries. *If it were up to me, the dangerous and immoral constraints of religion would be relieved of their hypocrisy, and dogmas of terror and subjugation would be abolished. Individualism is pivotal in this new world. Uniformity is for formal attire. Rules are for scientific principles.*

Freedom is about the individual, about respect and personal discipline. These will enrich each one of us in mind and body and allow us to be more productive, to be better at the things we pursue. And as we get better at what we do, we will learn humility. From humility comes amity.

Marta Sloane's speech played on Margaret's office computer while she looked up the last number she'd for Sam Cleave. She was excited to speak to him again after all this time, and could not help but cackle a little as she dialed his number. As the tone clicked into the first ring, Margaret was distracted by the bobbing frame of a male colleague just outside her window wall. He was waving wildly to get her attention, pointing to his watch and the flat screen of her computer.

"What the hell are you on about?" she said, hoping his aptitude for lip reading surpassed his hand signal skills. "I'm on the phone!"

Sam Cleave's phone went to voicemail, so Margaret stopped her call to open the door and hear what the clerk was on about. Jerking open the door with a hellish scowl, she snapped, "What in God's name is so important, Gary? I'm trying to get hold of Sam Cleave."

"That's just it!" Gary crowed. "Check the News. He's on the news, already in Germany, at the Heidelberg Hospital where the reporter said the fellow that crashed the German plane was!"

12

SELF-ASSIGNMENT

*M*argaret ran back into her office and switched the channel to SKY International. With eyes glued to the scenery on the screen, she sought between the strangers in the background to see if she could recognize her old colleague. Her focus was so fixed on this task that she hardly paid attention to the reporter's commentary. Here and there a word would simmer through the concoction of facts, striking her brain in the just the right place to memorize the overall story.

"Authorities are yet to apprehend the elusive murderer responsible for the deaths of two security officers three nights ago and another death last night. The identities of the deceased will be made available once the investigation by the Wiesloch branch of the criminal investigation unit under the Heidelberg Direktion is complete." Margaret suddenly discerned Sam amidst the onlookers behind the cordon signs and barriers. "My goodness, lad, how you have changed into...," she put on her glasses and leaned in to get a better look. Approvingly, she remarked, "Quite the good looking *ruggard* now that you are

a man, eh?" What a metamorphosis he had undergone! Now his dark hair was grown out just short of his shoulders, the ends flicking upward in a wild unkempt way that gave him an air of wayward sophistication.

He was dressed in a black leather coat and boots. Around his collar a roughly wrapped green Cashmere scarf adorned his dark features and equally shadowed clothing. In the misty grey of the German morning he was moving through the crowd to get a better look. Margaret noticed him speaking to a police officer who shook his head in response to whatever Sam was suggesting.

"Probably trying to get in, aren't you sweetie?" Margaret made a tiny smirk. "Well, you have not changed *that* much, have you?"

Behind him she recognized another man she'd often seen in press conferences and flashy university party footage sent over to the editing booth for news clips by the entertainment editor. The tall, white-haired man craned forward to scrutinize the scene next to Sam Cleave. He, too, was dressed impeccably. He had his glasses tucked inside his front coat pocket. His hands stayed hidden inside his pants pockets as he paced. She noticed his brown, Italian-cut, fleece wool blazer covering what she imagined had to be a concealed sidearm.

"David Purdue," she announced softly as the scene played out in two minimized versions in the glass of her spectacles. Her eyes moved away from the screen for a moment to shoot across the open plan office to see if Gradwell was stationary. He was quiet for once, perusing an article just brought in to him. Margaret scoffed and returned her gaze to the flat screen with a scoff. "Clearly you did not see that Cleave is still thick as thieves with Dave Purdue, did ya?" she chuckled.

"Two patients have been reported missing since this morning and police spokesperson..."

"What?" Margaret frowned. She'd heard *that* one. This was where she decided to perk her ears and pay attention to the report.

"...police have no idea how the two patients could have gotten out of the building with only one exit, an exit guarded by officers twenty-four hours a day. It led the authorities and hospital administration to believe that the two patients, Nina Gould and a burn victim only known as 'Sam,' could possibly still be at large inside the building. The reason for their absconding, though, remains a mystery."

"But Sam is outside the building, you idiots," Margaret scowled, thoroughly confused by the report. She was familiar with Sam Cleave's affiliation with Nina Gould, whom she'd once met briefly after a lecture on pre-World War II strategies visible in modern day politics; "Poor Nina. What happened to land them in the burn unit? My God. But Sam is..."

Margaret shook her head and moistened her lips with the tip of her tongue as she always did when she tried to solve a puzzle. Nothing made sense here; not the disappearance of patients through police barriers, not the mysterious deaths of three staff members without anyone as much as witnessing a suspect, and the strangest of all – the confusion of Nina's fellow patient being 'Sam' while Sam was standing outside among the onlookers...in plain sight.

The sharp deductive reasoning of Sam's old colleague

kicked in and she sank back in her chair as she watched Sam disappear off-screen along with the rest of the crowd. She steepled her fingers and stared blankly ahead of her, oblivious to the changing news reports.

"In plain sight," she said over and over as she articulated her formulas into different possibilities. "In plain sight..."

Margaret jumped up, knocking over her thankfully empty teacup and one of her Press Awards that had been lying on the edge of her desk. She gasped from her sudden epiphany, spurred on even further to speak to Sam. She wanted to get the long and short of the whole matter. By the bewilderment she felt, she knew there had to be several pieces of the puzzle she didn't have, pieces that only Sam Cleave could donate to her new pursuit of truth. And why wouldn't he? He would be only too happy to have someone with her logical intelligence to help him solve the mystery of Nina's disappearance.

It would be a pity if the beautiful little historian were still caught in the building with some kidnapper or madman. Such a thing almost guaranteed bad news, and she didn't want it to come to that at all, not if she could help it.

"Mr. Gradwell, I'm putting in a week for a story in Germany. Please arrange my away time allocation," she huffed as she swung open Gradwell's door, still busy putting on her coat in haste.

"What in the name of all things holy are you talking about, Margaret?" Gradwell exclaimed. He swung around in his chair.

"Sam Cleave is in Germany, Mr. Gradwell," she announced excitedly.

"Good! Then you can fill him in on the story that he's already there for," he shrieked.

"No, you don't understand. There is more, Mr. Gradwell, so much more! It would seem that Dr. Nina Gould is there too," she informed him through flushing as she rushed to do her belt. "And she is now reported missing by the authorities."

Margaret took a moment to catch her breath and see what her boss thought. He stared at her in disbelief for a second. Then he roared, "What the hell are you still doing here? Go and get Cleave. Let's expose the Krauts before someone else hops in a bloody suicide machine!"

13

THREE STRANGERS AND A MISSING HISTORIAN

"What do they say, Sam?" Purdue asked quietly as Sam joined him.

"They say two patients are missing since the early hours of this morning," Sam replied just as discreetly as the two walked away from the crowd to discuss their plans.

"We have to break Nina out before she becomes another target for this animal," Purdue insisted, his thumbnail placed askew between his front teeth as he mulled it over.

"Too late, Purdue," Sam announced with a sullen expression. He stopped walking and examined the skies above as if he were seeking help from some superior power. Purdue's light blue eyes stabbed at him in question, but Sam felt as if a stone had lodged itself in his stomach. Finally he gave a deep sigh and said, "Nina is missing."

Purdue did not process this immediately, maybe because it was the last thing he wanted to hear...next to tidings of her death, of course. Snapping at once out of his moment of thought, Purdue stared at Sam with a look of utmost intent.

"Use your mind control to get us some information. Come on, you used it to get me out of Sinclair." ~~he urged Sam,~~ But his friend only shook his head. "Sam? This is for the lady we both," he was reluctant to use the word he had in mind and tactfully replaced it with, "adore."

"I can't," Sam lamented. He looked distraught at this admittance, but there was no point in him perpetuating a fallacy. It would not benefit his ego or help anyone around him. "I l-lost...the...ability," he struggled.

For the first time since the Scottish festivities Sam said it out loud and it sucked. "I lost it, Purdue. When I fell over my own bloody feet running away from Giant Greta, or whatever her name was, my head struck a rock and, well," he shrugged and cast Purdue a look of terrible guilt. "I'm sorry, man. But I lost that thing I could do. Christ, when I had it I thought it was a spiteful curse – something to make my life miserable. Now that I don't have it...now that I truly *need* it, I wish it had not gone away."

"Splendid," Purdue moaned, his hand slipping over his brow and past his hairline to settle under the thick white of his hair. "Alright, let's think about this. Think. We've survived far worse than this instance without the help of some psychic trickery, right?"

"Aye," Sam agreed, still feeling like he'd let his side down.

"So we just have to employ old-fashioned tracking to find Nina," Purdue offered, trying hard to project his usual never-say-die attitude.

"What if she's still in there?" Sam shattered all illusions. "They say there is no way she could have walked out of here, so they reckon she might still be inside the building."

Sam had not been informed by the police officer he spoke to that a nurse had complained about being attacked the night before – a nurse who'd been robbed of her scrubs before she woke on the floor of the room wrapped in blankets.

"Then we have to get in. There's no point in looking for her all over Germany when we haven't properly covered the initial area and its vicinity," Purdue contemplated. His eyes recorded the proximity of the deployed officers and security people in plain clothes. With his tablet he covertly chronicled the scene, the floor access from outside the brown building, and the basic structure of its entrances and exits.

"Nice," Sam said, keeping a straight face and acting innocent. He whipped out a packet of smokes to help him think. Lighting his first one was like shaking hands with an old friend. Sam drew in the smoke and felt instantly at peace, focused, as if he had stepped back from it all to see the big picture. What he also saw, coincidentally, was the SKY International News van and three suspicious looking men loitering close to it. They seemed out of place somehow, but he couldn't put his finger on it.

Glancing at Purdue, Sam noticed that the white haired inventor was panning with his tablet, slowly moving it from right to left to capture the panorama.

"Purdue," Sam said through pursed lips, "go far left quickly. By the van. By the van there are three suspicious looking bastards. You see them?"

Purdue did as Sam suggested and filmed the three men in their early thirties, as far as he could tell. Sam was correct. It was clear they were not there to see what the commotion was about. Instead, they checked their watches all at once, hands on the buttons. One spoke as they waited.

"They're synchronizing their watches," Purdue remarked through barely moving lips.

"Aye," Sam concurred through a long stream of smoke that helped him observe without looking obvious. "What do you reckon – bomb?"

"Unlikely," Purdue replied evenly, his voice trailing like a distracted lecturer as he kept his tablet frame on the men. "They wouldn't remain in such close proximity."

"Unless they're suicidal," Sam retorted. Purdue peeked over the golden frame of his glasses, still keeping his tablet in place.

"Then they wouldn't have to synch their watches, would they?" he said impatiently. Sam had to concede. Purdue was right. They had to be there as observers, but of what? He pulled out another cigarette before even finishing the first.

"Gluttony is a deadly sin, you realize," Purdue teased, but Sam ignored him. He put out the butt of the exhausted fag and started walking in the direction of the three men before Purdue could react. He strolled casually across the flat grassland of untended land so as not to spook his targets. His German was appalling, so he decided to play himself this time. Perhaps if they thought him to be a dumb tourist they would be less reluctant to share.

"Hello, gents," Sam greeted cheerfully, placing his fag between his lips. "Don't suppose you have a light?"

They did not expect this. They peered with stunned expressions at the stranger who stood there grinning, looking stupid with his unlit cigarette.

"My wife went to have lunch with some other women on the tour and took my lighter with her." Sam plastered the excuse while taking special care to note their features and clothing. It was a journalist's prerogative, after all.

The red haired loiterer spoke to his friends in German. "Give him a light, for fuck's sake. Look how pathetic he looks." The other two chuckled in agreement and one stepped forward, flicking a flame for Sam. Now Sam realized that his distraction was ineffective, because all three still watched the hospital intently. "Da, Werner!" one exclaimed suddenly.

From the exit guarded by police, a small nurse stepped out and motioned for one of them to come. She had a brief word with the two guards at the door and they nodded satisfactorily.

"Kohl," the dark-haired one slapped the back of his hand against the arm of the red haired one.

"Warum nicht Himmelfarb?" Kohl protested, after which a quick fire argument ensued that was briskly settled between the three.

"Kohl! Sofort!" the dominant, dark-haired man reiterated forcefully.

In Sam's head the words struggled to find their way to his dictionary, but he presumed the first word was the lad's surname. The next word, he guessed, was along the lines of *making it quick*, but he was unsure.

"Oh, his wife is also giving the orders," Sam played dumb as he smoked lazily. "Mine is not as sweet..."

Franz Himmelfarb, with a nod from his associate, Dieter

Werner, interrupted Sam instantly. "Listen, friend, do you mind? We are on-duty officers trying to blend in and you are making things difficult for us. Our job is to make sure the killer inside the hospital does not escape unnoticed and for that, well, we need to not be bothered while doing our job."

"I understand. I'm sorry. I thought you were just a bunch of assholes waiting to steal petrol from the news van here. You looked the type," Sam replied with a somewhat deliberately snide attitude. He turned and walked away, ignoring the sound of one restraining the other. Sam glanced back to see them peering at him, which spurred him forward a bit more quickly toward Purdue's vicinity. He did not join his friend, however, and avoided visual association with him just in case the three hyenas were looking for a black sheep to single out. Purdue knew what Sam was doing. Sam's dark eyes widened slightly as their gazes met through the morning fog, furtively gesturing to Purdue that he should not engage him in conversation.

Purdue elected to return to the rental car with a few others who left the scene to get back to their day, while Sam stayed behind. He, on the other hand, joined up with a group of locals who had volunteered to help the police keep an eye out for any suspicious activity. It was merely his cover to keep his eye on the three underhanded boy scouts in their flannel shirts and windbreaker jackets. Sam called Purdue from his vantage point.

"Yes?" Purdue's voice came clearly over the phone.

"Military grade watches, all the exact same issue. These lads are from the armed forces," he reported as his eyes strayed all over the place to remain inconspicuous. "Also, names. Kohl, Werner and...uh...," he could not remember the third.

"Yes?" Purdue pressed as he entered the names into a German military personnel folder in the Defense Archives of the W.U.O.

"Shit," Sam frowned, wincing at his slacking faculty for memorizing details. "It's a longer surname."

"That, my friend, will not help me," Purdue mocked.

"I know! I know, for Christ's sake!" Sam seethed. He felt unusually impotent now that his once sharp abilities were challenged and found wanting. It was not the loss of his psychic ability that caused his new found self-loathing, but the frustration of not being able to joust as he once had when he was younger. "Heaven. It had something to do with heaven, I think. Jesus, I have to work on my German – and my goddamn memory."

"Engel, perhaps?" Purdue tried to help.

"No, too short," Sam contested. His eyes floated across the building, to the sky, dropping around the area of the three German soldiers. Sam gasped. They had vanished.

"Himmelfarb?" Purdue guessed.

"Aye, that's the one! That's the name!" Sam exclaimed in relief, but now he was concerned. "They're gone. They disappeared, Purdue. Fuck! I am just losing it all over the place, aren't I? I used to be able to tail a fart in a windstorm!"

Purdue was quiet, perusing the information he'd obtained from hacking into the off-limits covert files from the comfort of the car, while Sam stood in the cold morning air, waiting for something he did not even grasp.

"These lads are like a spider," Sam moaned as he searched

through the people with his eyes hidden under his whipping fringe. "They're threatening while you watch them, but it's so much worse when you don't know where they've gone."

"Sam," Purdue spoke suddenly, starting the journalist who was convinced that he was being stalked for an ambush. "They are all airmen in the German Luftwaffe, section Leo 2."

"And what does that mean? Are they pilots?" Sam asked. He was almost disappointed.

"Not quite. They are a bit more specialized," Purdue clarified. "Come back to the car. You'll want to hear this over a double rum on the rocks."

14

CONFUSION IN MANNHEIM

*N*ina woke up on the couch, feeling as if someone had implanted a rock inside her skull and merely pushed her brain aside to ache. She was reluctant to open her eyes. It would be too hard on her cheer to find that she had gone completely blind, but it was just too unnatural not to. Carefully she allowed her lids to flutter apart. Nothing had changed since the day before, for which she was exceedingly grateful.

Toast and coffee permeated the living room where she had keeled over after a very long walk with her hospital partner, 'Sam'. He still could not remember his name and she still could not get used to calling him Sam. But she had to admit, apart from all the discrepancies about him, thus far he had helped her stay undetected from the authorities, authorities who would have loved to have thrown her back into the hospital where a madman had already come to say hi.

They'd spent the whole day before on foot, trying to reach Mannheim before dark. Neither had any credentials or money on them, so Nina had to play the pity card to get a free lift for them both from Mannheim to Dillenburg north from there. Unfortunately, the sixty-two-year-old lady Nina was trying to convince had felt it would be better for the two tourists to get a meal, warm shower and a good night's sleep. And this was why she had spent the night on a couch, playing host to two large cats and an embroidered pillow that reeked of stale cinnamon.*Geez, I have to get hold of Sam. My Sam,* she reminded herself as she sat up. Her lower back had stepped into the ring with her hips and Nina felt like an old woman, full of aches and pains. Her eyes had not deteriorated, but it was still a problem for her to act normally when she could hardly see. On top of that, both she and her new friend had to keep from being recognized as the two patients missing from Heidelberg's medical facility. It was particularly hard for Nina, as she had to pretend not to have sore skin and a devastating fever most of the time.

"Good morning!" the kind hostess said from the doorway. With a spatula in one hand she asked in a disturbingly heavy German drawl, "Do you want eggs with your toast, Schatz?"

Nina nodded with a goofy smile, wondering if she looked half as bad as she felt. Before she could ask where the bathroom was, the lady had vanished back into the lime green kitchen where the smell of margarine joined the array of flavors wafting into Nina's keen nose. Suddenly it hit her. *Where is Other Sam?*

She recalled the hostess giving them each a couch to sleep on the night before, but his was vacant. Not that she wasn't relieved to be alone for a bit, but he knew the countryside better than her and he had been serving as her eyes thus far. Nina was still in her jeans and shirt from the hospital, having discarded the scrubs just outside the Heidelberg facility once the majority of eyes were off them.

Throughout the entire time she shared with the other Sam, Nina could not help but wonder how he had passed as Dr. Hilt before he left the hospital after her. Surely the officers on guard would know that a man with a burned face could not possibly have been the late doctor, regardless of a clever disguise and a nametag. Of course, she had no way of discerning his features with the state that her sight was in.

Nina pulled her sleeves over her reddened forearms, feeling the nausea grip her body.

"Toilet?" she managed to call out around the doorway of the kitchen, before bolting down the short hallway the lady pointed to with the spatula. Barely at the door, the waves of convulsions attacked Nina and she quickly slammed the door shut to purge. It was no secret that acute radiation syndrome was causing her gastrointestinal malady, but not receiving treatment for this and the other symptoms only exacerbated her circumstances.

When she had vomited herself even weaker, Nina timidly appeared from the bathroom and made her way to the couch where she'd slept. Another problem was keeping her balance without holding on to the wall as she went. Throughout the small house Nina realized the rooms were all unoccupied. Could he *have left me here? The bastard!* She frowned under the spell of the climbing fever she could not fight anymore. With the added disorientation of her flawed eyes, she strained just to make it to the warped object she hoped to be the large couch. Nina's bare feet dragged along the carpet as the woman rounded the corner to bring her some breakfast.

"Oh! Mein Gott!" she shrieked in panic at the sight of the small frame of her guest collapsing. Briskly the lady of the house set the tray down on the table and rushed to come to Nina's aid. "My darling, are you alright?"

Nina could not tell her that she had been in hospital. In fact, she could hardly tell her anything. Spinning in her skull, her brain hissed while her breath felt like an open oven door. Her eyes rolled back as she went limp in the arms of the lady. Soon after Nina came to again, her face feeling ice cold under trickles of sweat beads. A washcloth was on her forehead and she could feel an uncomfortable fumbling at her thighs, which alarmed her into a swift upright position. An indifferent cat met her gaze as her hand grabbed at the furry body and released immediately afterward. "Oh," was all Nina could manage, and laid back down.

"How are you feeling?" the lady asked.

"I must be getting sick from the cold here in a strange country," Nina blabbered softly to maintain her deceit. *Yeah right,* her inner voice mocked. *A Scot recoiling at German autumn. Good one!*

Then her hostess said the golden words. "Liebchen, is there someone I should call to come and get you? Husband? Family?" Nina's moist, pallid face lit up with hope. "Yes, please!"

"Your friend here did not even say goodbye this morning. When I got up to drive you two to town he was just gone. Did you two have a fight?"

"No, he said he was in a hurry to get to his brother's house. Maybe he thought I would hold him up, being sick," Nina answered, and realized that her hypothesis was probably precisely true. When the two of them spent the day walking along the backcountry road outside of Heidelberg, they did not exactly bond. But he did tell her what he could remember about his identity. At the time, Nina had found the other Sam's memory remarkably selective, but she had not wanted to rock the boat while she was this dependent on his guidance and tolerance.

She remembered that he did wear a long white coat, but other than that it was almost impossible to see his face, even if he still had one. What vexed her a bit was the lack of shock expressed by the sight of him wherever they asked for directions or interacted with others. Surely, had they seen a man whose face and torso had been reduced to toffee, people would make some sort of sound or exclaim some kind of sympathetic word? But they responded in a trivial fashion, showing no sign of concern for the man's clearly fresh injuries.

"What happened to your cell phone?" the lady asked her - a perfectly normal question to which Nina effortlessly shot the most obvious lie.

"I was robbed. My bag with my phone, money, all of that. Gone. I suppose they knew I was a tourist and targeted me," Nina explained as she took the woman's phone with a nod of thanks. She dialed the number she had so well memorized. When the phone rang on the other end of the line, it gave Nina a jump in energy and just a little warmth in her belly.

"Cleave."*My God, what a beautiful word,* Nina thought, suddenly feeling much safer than she had in a long time. How long since she had heard the voice of her old friend, occasional lover and periodic colleague? Her heart jumped.

Nina had not seen Sam since he was abducted by the Order of the Black Sun while they were on an excursion seeking the famed 18th Century Amber Room in Poland almost two months ago.

"S-Sam?" she said, almost laughing.

"Nina?" he cried out. "Nina? Is that you?"

"Aye. How are you doing?" she smiled weakly. Her body ached all over and she could hardly sit up.

"Jesus Christ, Nina! Where are you? Are you in danger?" he asked frantically through the heavy hum of a moving car.

"I'm alive, Sam. Barely, though. But I'm safe. With a lady in Mannheim here in Germany. Sam? Can you come and get me?" her voice cracked. The request hit Sam in the heart. Such a feisty, intelligent and independent woman was not likely to beg for rescue like a small child.

"Of course I'll come to get you! Mannheim is a short drive from where I am. Give me the address and we'll come get you," Sam exclaimed on excitedly. "Oh my God, you have no idea how happy we are that you're okay!"

"What is all this *we*?" she asked. "And why are you in Germany?"

"To get you to a hospital back home, naturally. We saw on the news that there was a heap of hell loose where Detlef left you. And when we got here you were missing! I cannot believe this," he raved, his laughter rife with relief.

"I'll give you to the dear lady who took me in for the address. See you soon, okay?" Nina replied through her heavy-laden breath and gave the phone to her hostess before falling into a deep sleep.

When Sam had said 'we', she'd had a bad feeling that it meant he'd sprung Purdue from whatever deserving cage he'd been imprisoned in after Detlef had cold-cocked him beneath Chernobyl. But with the illness ripping through her system like a punishment from the Morphine god deserted in her wake, she did not care for the moment. All she wanted to do was fade away into the arms of whatever awaited.

She could still hear the lady explaining what the house looked like when she abandoned control and slipped into a feverish slumber.

15

BAD MEDICINE

*S*ister Barken sat on the thick leather of the vintage office chair with her elbows resting on her knees. Under the monotonous buzz of the luminescent light her hands cradled the sides of her head as she listened to the administrator's account of Dr. Hilt's demise. The stout nursing sister wept for the doctor she had known for barely seven months. She had not gotten along smoothly with him, but she was a compassionate woman who truly felt sorry about the man's death.

"The funeral is tomorrow," the administrator said before she left the office.

"I saw this on the news, you know, about the murders. Dr. Fritz told me not to come in unnecessarily. He did not want me to be in danger too," she told her subordinate, Nurse Marx. "Marlene, you must ask for a transfer. I cannot stand worrying about you every time I'm off duty."

"Don't worry about me, Sister Barken," Marlene Marx smiled, passing her one of the cups of instant soup she'd prepared. "I think whoever did this must have had a specific reason, you know? Like a target that was already here."

"You don't think...?" Sister Barken gawked at Nurse Marx.

"Dr. Gould," Nurse Marx affirmed the Sister's fears. "I think it was someone who wanted to kidnap her and now that they have taken her," she shrugged, "the danger to staff and patients is gone. I mean, I bet the poor people who died only met their end because they got in the killer's way, you know? They probably tried to stop him."

"I understand that theory, sweetheart, but why then is the 'Sam' patient also missing?" asked Sister Barken. By the look on Marlene's face she could see that the young nurse had not yet thought of that. In silence she sipped her soup.

"So sad that he took Dr. Gould, though," Marlene lamented. "She had been very ill and her eyes were only getting worse, poor woman. On another note, my mother was furious when she heard about Dr. Gould's abduction. She was angry that all this time was right here in my care I didn't tell her."

"Oh boy," Sister Barken empathized with her. "She must have given you hell. I've seen that woman upset and she scares even me."

The two dared to have a giggle in this bleak situation. Dr. Fritz entered the Third Floor nurse's office with a folder under his arm. His face was serious, halting their meager joviality instantly. Something that resembled sorrow or disappointment shown in his eyes as he made himself a cup of coffee.

"Guten Morgen, Dr. Fritz," the young nurse said to break the awkward silence.

He didn't answer her. Sister Barken was surprised at his rudeness and used her authoritarian voice to shake the man to a measure of decency with the same greeting, only a few decibels louder. Dr. Fritz jumped around, jolted from his comatose state of thought.

"Oh, I'm sorry, ladies," he gasped. "Good morning. Good morning," he nodded to each, wiping his sweaty palm on his coat before stirring his coffee.

It was very unlike Dr. Fritz to act this way. To most women who encountered him, he was Germany's medical field's answer to George Clooney. His confident charm was his power, only trumped by his medical prowess. Yet here he stood in the humble Third Floor office with sweaty palms and an apologetic disposition that baffled both ladies.

Sister Barken and Nurse Marx quietly exchanged frowns before the robust veteran stood up to wash her cup. "Dr. Fritz, what has upset you? Nurse Marx and I volunteer to find whoever upset you and treat them to a free barium enema with some of my special Chai tea...straight from the pot!"

Nurse Marx could not help but choke on her soup from unexpected laughter, although she was not sure how the doctor would react. Her wide eyes stared stiffly at her superior's in an imperceptible reprimand as her jaw hung open in amusement. Sister Barken was unperturbed. She was very comfortable using humor to elicit information, even personal and highly emotional information.

Dr. Fritz smiled and shook his head. He enjoyed the approach, although what he was harboring was by no means worthy of a jest.

"Much as I appreciate the valiant gesture, Sister Barken, my distress is not caused by a person as much as by a person's fate," he said in his most civilized tone.

"May I inquire of whom?" Sister Barken pried.

"Actually, I insist," he replied. "Both of you treated Dr. Gould, so it would be more than appropriate for you to know the results of Nina's tests."

Both of Marlene's hands lifted silently to her face, covering her mouth and nose in a gesture of anticipation. Sister Barken understood Nurse Marx's reaction, as she herself did not feel too positive about the news. Besides, if it had Dr. Fritz in a bubble of quiet ignorance to the world it had to be hefty.

"It is a setback, especially after she had been healing so rapidly at first," he started, tightening his grip on the file. "The tests show a significant deterioration in her blood work. Cellular damage was too severe for the time it took for her to be admitted for treatment."

"Oh sweet Jesus," Marlene whined in her hands. Tears filled her eyes, but Sister Barken's face remained in the expression she was trained to receive bad news.

Blank.

"What kind of level are we looking at?" Sister Barken asked.

"Well, her intestines and lungs seem to be bearing the brunt of the developing cancer, but there is also clear indication that she had suffered some minute neurological damage that is probably the cause of her deteriorating eye sight, Sister Barken. She was only tested, so I will not be able to make a definite diagnosis until I get to examine her again."

In the background, Nurse Marx was whimpering softly at the news, but she tried her best to compose herself and not allow a patient to influence her so personally. She knew it was not professional to cry over a patient, but this was not just any patient. It was Dr. Nina Gould, her inspiration and an acquaintance she had a very soft spot for.

"I just hope we can find her soon, so that we can bring her back in before it gets any worse than it has to be. We simply cannot just discard hope like this, even though," he said as he looked down at the young, crying nurse, "it's pretty hard to stay positive."

"Dr. Fritz, the German Air Force Commander is sending a man to interview you sometime today," Dr. Fritz's assistant announced from the doorway. She did not have time to ask why Nurse Marx was in tears, as she was in a hurry to return to the small office of Dr. Fritz that she was in charge of.

"Who?" he asked, confidence returned.

"He says his name is Werner. Dieter Werner from the public office of the German Air Force. It's regarding the burn victim that disappeared from the hospital. I checked – he has military authority to be here on behalf of Lieutenant-General Harold Meier." She practically recite all of this in one single breath.

"I don't know what to tell these people anymore," Dr. Fritz complained. "They cannot clean up their own mess and now they come and waste my time with..." and off he went muttering furiously. His assistant gave the two nurses one more glance before rushing after her boss.

"What is that about?" Sister Barken sighed. "I'm glad I'm not in the poor doctor's shoes. Come on, Nurse Marx. Time for our rounds." She resumed her normal austere form of command just to establish that work time had begun. And with her usual stern annoyance she added, "And wipe your eyes, for Pete's sake, Marlene, before patients think you are as high as they are!"

SEVERAL HOURS later Nurse Marx took a breather. She had just emerged from the Maternity Ward, where she had been donating her shift time for two hours each day. Two of the regular maternity nurses had put in compassionate leave after the recent murders, so the ward was a bit short staffed. In the nurses' office she took the weight off her sore feet and she listened to the promising rumble of the kettle.

While she waited, a few rays of gilded light illuminated the table and chairs in front of the small fridge and led her gaze along the precise lines of the furniture. In her state of fatigue it brought to mind the sad news of earlier. Right there on the smooth surface of the off-white table she could still see the folder of Dr. Nina Gould, lying there like any other chart she might read. Only this one had a smell to it. A rotten smell of decay permeated from it, choking Nurse Marx until she jumped from the horrid dream with a sudden flail of her hand. She almost sent her teacup flying to the hard floor, but caught it just in time, employing those adrenaline-fuelled reflexes of a sudden start.

"Oh my goodness!" she whispered in a puff of panic, holding the porcelain cup tightly. Her eyes fell on the barren top of the table where there was no file in sight. To her relief it had just been an ugly mirage of a recent shock, but she wished sorely that that was the case with the actual news contained therein. Why could that, too, not just have been a bad dream? Poor Nina!

Marlene Marx felt her eyes moisten again, but this time it was not for Nina's condition. It was because she had no idea whether the beautiful, dark-haired historian was even alive, let alone where she'd been taken by the stonehearted villain.

16

MERRY MEET/ UN-MERRY PART

"Just got a call from an old colleague of mine at the Edinburgh Post, Margaret Crosby," Sam shared, still staring at his phone a little nostalgically just after he got into the rental car with Purdue. "She's on her way here to offer me a co-authorship on the investigation concerning the German Air Force's involvement in some sort of scandal."

"Sounds like a good story. You should do it, old chum. I smell an international conspiracy here, but I'm no news hound," said Purdue as they made their way to Nina's temporary sanctuary.

When Sam and Purdue pulled up in front of the house they were directed to, the place looked ghastly. Although the modest little house had been recently painted, the garden was wild. The contrast between the two made the house stand out. Bushes with thorns hugged the beige exterior walls under a black roof. The chimney's pale, pink paint chips showed the decay from before the paint job. Smoke slithered upward from it like a lazy, grey dragon, blending in with the cold, monochrome clouds of the overcast day.

The house stood at the end of a small street near a lake, which only added to the desolate loneliness of the place. As the two men stepped out of the car, Sam could see a twitch in one of the windows as the curtains were being disturbed.

"We've been detected," Sam announced to his companion. Purdue nodded, his tall body towering above the frame of the car door. His fair hair fluffed in the moderate wind as he watched the front door crack open. A podgy, kind face peered from behind the door.

"Frau Bauer?" asked Purdue from the other side of the vehicle.

"Herr Cleave?" she smiled.

Purdue pointed to Sam and smiled.

"Go, Sam. I don't think Nina should see me right off the bat, you know?" Sam understood. His friend had a fair point. After all, he and Nina did not part on the best of terms on account of Purdue hunting her in the dark, threatening to kill her and all that.

When Sam skipped up the front steps to where the lady was holding the door open, he could not help but wish he could stay a while. The interior of the house smelled divine with the blended scent of flowers, coffee and a faint reminiscence of what could have been French toast a few hours ago.

"Thank you," he told Frau Bauer.

"She is through here. She's been sleeping since you and I spoke on the phone," she informed Sam, shamelessly staring at his rugged good looks. It gave him an uncomfortable, prison-rape feeling, but Sam pinned his attention on Nina. Her small frame was curled up under a pile of blankets, some of which turned into cats when he pulled them away to see Nina's face.

Sam did not show it, but he was shocked to see how bad she looked. Her lips were blue upon her pasty face, hair clinging to her temples as she breathed hoarsely.

"Is she a smoker?" Frau Bauer asked. "Her lungs sound terrible. She refused to let me call the hospital before you'd seen her. Should I call them now?"

"Not yet," Sam said quickly. On the phone Frau Bauer had told him about the man who had accompanied Nina, and Sam reckoned it was the other missing person from the hospital. "Nina," he said softly, running his fingertips along her crown and repeating her name a little louder each time. Eventually her eyes opened and she smiled, "Sam."*Jesus! What's wrong with her eyes?* he thought with a jolt of dread at the light sheet of cataracts that had made cobwebs all over her eyes.

"Hey beautiful," he answered, kissing her forehead. "How did you know it was me?"

"Are you kidding me?" she said slowly. "Your voice is burned into my mind...just like your scent."

"My scent?" he asked.

"Marlboro and attitude," she jested. "Christ, I'd kill for a fag right now."

Frau Bauer choked on her tea. Sam chuckled. Nina coughed.

"We were worried sick, love," Sam said. "Let us take you to the hospital. Please."

Nina's damaged eyes bolted open. "No."

"Things have calmed down there now." He was trying to dupe her, but Nina would have none of it.

"I'm not stupid, Sam. I've been following the news from here. They haven't caught that son of a bitch yet, and the last time we spoke he made it clear that I was playing on the wrong side of the fence," she wheezed hastily.

"Alright, alright. Calm down a little and tell me exactly what that means, because to me it sounds as if you had direct contact with the killer," Sam replied, trying to keep his voice void of the true terror he felt for what she was insinuating.

"Tea or coffee, Herr Cleave?" the kind hostess asked quickly.

"Doro makes a mean cinnamon tea, Sam. Try it," Nina suggested wearily.

Sam nodded amicably, sending the eager German woman into the kitchen. He was concerned about Purdue sitting in the car during the time it would take to get to the bottom of Nina's current situation. Nina faded into semi-sleep again, lulled by the Bundesliga war on television. Concerned for her life in the midst of her juvenile tantrum, Sam sent Purdue a text.

She is stubborn, as we thought.

Deathly ill. Any ideas?

He sighed, waiting for any ideas of how to get Nina to a hospital before her obstinacy signed off on her mortality. Naturally, non-violent coercion was the only way with someone delirious and pissed at the world, but he feared that would alienate Nina further, especially from Purdue. His phone's tone shattered the monotony of the commentator on TV, waking Nina. Sam looked down to where he was concealing his phone.

Offer a different hospital?

Otherwise knock her out with loaded sherry.

On the latter Sam knew Purdue was being facetious. The former, however, was an excellent thought. Immediately after the first message came the next.

Universitätsklinikum Mannheim.

Theresienkrankenhaus.

A deep scowl fell into Nina's clammy forehead. "What the fuck is that constant ruckus?" she murmured through the spinning funhouse of her fever. "Make it stop! Geezusss..."

Sam muted his phone to appease the vexed woman he was trying to save. Frau Bauer came in with a tray. "I'm sorry, Frau Bauer," Sam apologized very quietly. "We will be out of your hair in just a few minutes."

"Don't be crazy," she rasped in her hefty accent. "Take your time. Just make sure Nina gets to the hospital soon. She looks bad to me."

"Danke," Sam replied. He took a sip of the tea, trying not to scald his mouth. Nina was right. The hot beverage was as close to ambrosia as he could imagine.

"Nina?" Sam dared again. "We have to get out of here. Your pal from the hospital deserted you, so I don't exactly trust him. If he comes back with a few friends we're in trouble."

Nina opened her eyes. Sam felt a bolt of sorrow cripple him as she looked past his face into the space behind him. "I'm not going back."

"No, no, you don't have to," he soothed. "We will take you to a local hospital here in Mannheim, love."

"No, Sam!" she pleaded. Her chest was heaving alarmingly as her hands tried to find the hair on her face that bothered her. Nina's thin fingers folded against her skull as she tried to remove the clingy tresses repeatedly, getting more annoyed every time she failed. Sam did it for her while she looked at what she thought was his face. "Why can't I go back home? Why can't I be treated in a hospital in Edinburgh?"

Nina suddenly gasped and held her breath, her nostrils wagging slightly. Frau Bauer was standing at the door with a guest she had gone to fetch.

"You can."

"Purdue!" Nina gagged, trying to swallow with her dry throat.

"You can be transported to the medical facility of your choice in Edinburgh, Nina. Just allow us to get you to an ER nearby to stabilize you. As soon as they do, Sam and I will fly you home immediately. I promise you," said Purdue informed her.

He kept his voice soft and even, so as not to excite her nerves. His words were bathed in positive tones of resolution. Purdue knew he had to give her what she desired without any talk of Heidelberg as a whole.

"What do you say, love?" Sam smiled, stroking her hair. "You don't want to die in Germany, do you?" He looked up apologetically to the German hostess, but she only smiled and waved it away.

"You tried to kill me!" Nina growled into somewhere all around her. She could hear where he was standing at first, but Purdue's voice moved as he spoke, so she lashed out anyway.

"He was programmed, Nina, to follow the commands of that Black Sun twat. Come on, you know Purdue would never hurt you intentionally," Sam tried, but she was panting wildly. They could not tell if Nina was furious or terrified, but her hands felt around madly until she found Sam's arm. She clutched onto him as her milky eyes shot from side to side.

"Please, God, don't let this be Purdue," she said.

Sam shook his head in disappointment as Purdue walked out of the house. There was no doubt that Nina's remark had hit him very hard this time. Frau Bauer looked sympathetic as she watched the tall, fair-haired man leave. Finally, Sam decided to get Nina up.

"Come," he said, gently handling her frail body.

"Keep the blankets. I can knit more," Frau Bauer smiled.

"Thank you so much. You've been a great, great help," Sam told the hostess as he lifted Nina into his arms and carried her out to the car. Purdue's face was plain and expressionless while Sam loaded the sleeping Nina into the car.

"Right, she's in," Sam announced light heartedly, trying to comfort Purdue without getting soppy. "I think we'll need to go back to Heidelberg to get her file from her previous doctor after she is admitted in Mannheim."

"You can go. I'm returning to Edinburgh as soon as we sort Nina out." Purdue's words left a hole in Sam.

Sam frowned, dumbfounded. "But you said you would fly her to a hospital there." He understood Purdue's frustration, but it was not worth playing with Nina's life.

"I know what I said, Sam," he said harshly. The empty look was back; that same look he had had at Sinclair, when he told Sam that he was beyond help. Purdue started the car. "I also know what *she* said."

17

DOUBLE SUBTERFUGE

*I*n the top office of the Fifth Floor, Dr. Fritz was meeting with an esteemed representative of the Tactical Air Force Wing 34 Büchel Air Base on behalf of the high commander of the Luftwaffe, who was currently being hounded by the press and family of the missing airman.

"Thank you for seeing me unannounced, Dr. Fritz," Werner said cordially, disarming the medical specialist with his charisma. "The Lieutenant-General asked me to come because he is inundated with visits and legal threats at the moment, as I am sure you can appreciate."

"Yes. Please sit down, Mr. Werner," Dr. Fritz said abruptly. "As I am sure you can appreciate, I also have a tight schedule, what with critical and terminal patients to see to without unnecessary interruptions of my daily work."

Werner sneered as he sat down, put off not only by the doctor's looks but also by his reluctance to see him. However, when it came to missions, such things were not in the least troublesome to Werner. He was there to retrieve as much information about Airman Löwenhagen and the extent of his injuries as he could. Dr. Fritz would have no choice but to assist him in finding the burn victim, particularly under the pretense that they wished to set his family at ease. Of course, in actual fact, he was fair game.

What Werner also did not bring to the fore was the fact that the commander did not trust the medical facility enough to merely accept information. He was keeping well under wraps that, while he was engaging Dr. Fritz on the Fifth Floor, his two colleagues were sweeping the building with a well-trained, fine-toothed comb for the possible presence of the pest. Each scoured the area individually, moving up one flight of fire stairs and down the next. They knew they only had a certain amount of time to complete the search before Werner would be done interviewing the presiding physician. Once they were sure Löwenhagen was not in the hospital, they could spread out their search to other possible locations.

It was just after breakfast time when Dr. Fritz asked Werner a more pressing question.

"Lieutenant Werner, if I may," his words twisted sarcastically. "How is it that your squadron commander is not here to speak to me about this? I think we should cut the bullshit, you and I. We both know why Schmidt is after the young airman, but what does it have to do with you?"

"Orders. I am but a representative, Dr. Fritz. But my report will reflect accurately how swiftly you assisted us," Werner replied firmly. But in truth he had no idea why his commander, Captain Gerhard Schmidt, was sending him and his associates out after the pilot. The three of them assumed they were out to exterminate the pilot just for embarrassing the Luftwaffe when he crashed one of their obscenely expensive Tornado fighter planes. "Once we have what we want," he bluffed, "we will all receive a reward for it."

"The mask does not belong to him," Dr. Fritz declared defiantly. "You go and tell Schmidt that, errand boy."

Werner's face went ashen. Rage filled him, but he was not there to disassemble a medical professional. The doctor's blatant derogatory derision was an undeniable call to war, which Werner mentally placed on his to-do list for later. But for now he was focused on this juicy morsel of information Captain Schmidt had not counted upon.

"I shall inform him of just that, sir." Werner's clear, narrowed eyes pierced through Dr. Fritz. A smirk formed on the fighter pilot's face while the clatter of dishes and the chatter of hospital staff drowned their words of secret jousting. "Once the mask is found, I will be sure to invite you to the ceremony." Again Werner was prying, trying to throw in keywords untraceable to specific meaning.

Dr. Fritz laughed out loud. He slammed the desk in amusement. "Ceremony?"

Werner feared that he had ruined the play for an instant, but it soon benefitted his curiosity. "Did he tell you that? Ha! Did he tell you that you need a ceremony to assume the face of the victim? Oh, my boy!" Dr. Fritz sniffed as he wiped tears of amusement from the corners of his eyes.

Werner was elated at the doctor's arrogance, so he milked it by discarding his ego and apparently admitting he had been fooled. Looking utterly disappointed, he proceeded to answer, "He lied to me?" His voice was down, barely louder than a whisper.

"That's right, Lieutenant. The Babylonian Mask is not cere-monial. Schmidt is deceiving you to keep you from profiting from it. Let's face it, it is an extremely valuable piece for the highest bidder," Dr. Fritz spilled eagerly.

"If it is so valuable, why did you give it back to Löwen-hagen?" Werner ventured deeper.

Dr. Fritz stared at him in utter befuddlement.

"Löwenhagen. Who is Löwenhagen?"

WHILE NURSE MARX was busy clearing out the last of the used medical waste from her rounds, the faint sound of the ringing phone in the nurses' station drew her attention. With a laborious groan she jogged to answer it, since none of her colleagues were finished with their patients yet. It was the reception desk on the Ground Floor.

"Marlene, there is someone here to see Dr. Fritz, but there is no answer in his office," the receptionist said. "He says it is very urgent and lives depend on it. Can you put the doctor on the line?"

"Um, he's not nearby. I'd have to go and look for him. What is it about?"

The receptionist answered in a subdued voice, "He insists that if he does not see Dr. Fritz, Nina Gould will die."

"Oh my God!" Nurse Marx gasped. "He has Nina?"

"I don't know. He just said his name is...*Sam*," whispered the receptionist, a close acquaintance of Nurse Marx who knew about the burn victim's assumed name.

Nurse Marx's body went numb. Her adrenaline edged her forward and she waved her arm to get the attention of the Third Floor security man. He came running from the far side of the hallway, hand on his holster, passing visitors and staff on the pristine floor that mirrored his reflection.

"Okay, tell him I'll come to get him and I'll take him up to see Dr. Fritz," Nurse Marx said. After she hung up, she told the security officer, "There is a man downstairs, one of the two missing patients. He says he must see Dr. Fritz or the other missing patient will die. I need you to come with me to apprehend him."

The security guard released the strap of his holster with a click and nodded. "Got it. But you stay behind me." He radioed his unit to report that he was about to arrest a possible suspect and proceeded with Nurse Marx to the reception area. Marlene felt her heart racing, terrified, but excited about the development. If she could be part of the arrest of the suspect who had kidnapped Dr. Gould, she would be a hero.

With two other officers flanking them, Nurse Marx and the security man descended the stairs to the Ground Floor. As they reached the landing and turned the corner, Nurse Marx peeked eagerly past the huge officer to see the burn unit patient she knew so well. But he was nowhere to be seen.

"Nurse, which man is it?" asked the officer, while the other two readied themselves to evacuate the area. Nurse Marx just shook her head. "I don't...I don't see him." Her eyes examined every single man in the lobby, but there was nobody with burn injuries on their face and chest anywhere. "This cannot be," she said. "Wait, I'll call out his name."Standing amidst all the people in the lobby and waiting area Nurse Marx stood still and called out, "Sam! Can you come with me to see Dr. Fritz, please?"

The receptionist shrugged at Marlene and said, "What the hell are you doing? He is right here!" She was pointing at the handsome, dark-haired man in the posh coat waiting at the side of the counter. He approached her immediately, smiling. The officers drew their guns, stopping Sam in his tracks. At the same time, the onlookers caught their breath; some disappeared around corners.

"What is going on?" Sam asked.

"You're not Sam," Nurse Marx frowned.

"Nurse, is this the kidnapper or not?" the one officer asked impatiently.

"What?" Sam exclaimed, scowling. "I am Sam Cleave, looking for Dr. Fritz."

"Do you have Dr. Nina Gould?" the officer asked.

In the background of their discussion the nurse gasped. *The* Sam Cleave, right here in front of her.

"Aye," Sam started, but before he could utter another word they lifted their guns in a straight aim at him. "But I did not kidnap her! Jesus! Put your guns away, you idiots!"

"That is not the correct way to speak to an officer of the law, son," the other officer reminded Sam.

"I'm sorry," Sam said quickly. "Alright? I'm sorry, but you have to hear me out. Nina is my friend and she is currently undergoing medical care in Mannheim at the Theresien hospital. They need her folder or file, whatever, and she sent me to see her attending doctor to get that information. That is all! That is all I am here for, understand?"

"Identification," the security guard demanded. "Slowly."

Sam refrained from poking fun at the officer's FBI-movie moves, just in case they were trigger-happy. Carefully he opened the flap of his coat and retrieved his passport.

"There you go. Sam Cleave. See?" Nurse Marx came out from behind the officer, apologetically putting out her hand to Sam.

"I am so sorry for the misunderstanding," she told Sam, and repeated the same to the officers. "You see, the other patient that went missing with Dr. Gould was also called Sam. Obviously I immediately thought it was *that* Sam wanting to see the doctor. And when he said Dr. Gould could die..."

"Yes, yes, we get the picture, Nurse Marx," the security man sighed, holstering his gun. The other two were equally frustrated, but they had no choice but to follow suit.

18

UNMASKED

"*As* you were," Sam jested as he was given back his credentials. The flushing young nurse lifted her open hand in a grateful gesture to them as they walked away, feeling dreadfully sheepish.

"Mr. Cleave, it is an honor to meet you." She smiled, shaking Sam's hand.

"Call me Sam," he flirted, deliberately looking intensely into her eyes. Besides, an ally could help his mission along; not only in obtaining Nina's folder, but also in getting to the bottom of the recent incidents at the hospital and perhaps even the air base in Büchel.

"I am so sorry for screwing up like this. The other patient she disappeared with was also called Sam," she explained.

"Aye, my darling, I caught that the other time. No need to apologize. It was an honest mistake." They got an elevator to the Fifth Floor. *A mistake that almost cost me my bloody life!*

In the elevator with two radiology technicians and the

gushing Nurse Marx, Sam pushed the awkwardness from his mind. They were silently staring at him. For a split second Sam contemplated spooking the German ladies with a remark on how he once saw a Swedish porn flick start much in the same fashion. The doors opened on the Second Floor and Sam caught a glimpse of a white sign on the hallway wall reading "X-ray 1 & 2" in red lettering. The two radiology technicians breathed out for the first time only after they'd stepped out of the lift. Sam could hear their giggling die down as the silver doors slid together again.

Nurse Marx wore a smirk and her eyes stayed glued to the floor, prompting the journalist to relieve her of her discomfiture. He breathed out hard, looking at the light above them. "So, Nurse Marx, is Dr. Fritz a radiology specialist?"

Her posture straightened up instantly like a loyal soldier. From Sam's knowledge of body language he realized that the nurse harbored an undying reverence or desire for the doctor in question. "No, but he is a veteran physician who lectures at global medical conferences on several scientific subjects. Let me say – he knows a little about every disease, where other doctors specialize in just one and know nothing about the rest. He took very good care of Dr. Gould. You can be assured. In fact, he was the only one who picked up on th..."

Nurse Marx swallowed her words immediately, almost spilling the cancerous news she'd been stunned by just that morning.

"What?" he asked kindly.

"All I meant to say is that whatever is plaguing Dr. Gould, Dr. Fritz will figure it out," she said, pressing her lips together. "Ah! Here we go!" she smiled, delighted at their well-timed arrival on the Fifth Floor.

She led Sam out to the Administrative wing of the Fifth Floor, past the archives office, and a staff tearoom. While they walked, Sam enjoyed periodical sights from the identical square windows that lined the off-white hall. Every time the wall gave way to a blinded window, the sun would reach through and warm Sam's face, showing him an aerial view over the local surroundings. He wondered where Purdue was. He'd left Sam the car and had taken a taxi to the airport without much explanation. That was another matter for Sam to carry unresolved deep inside his psyche until he had time to deal with it.

"Dr. Fritz should be done with his interview by now," Nurse Marx informed Sam as they neared the closed door. She briefly explained about the Air Force commander sending an emissary to speak to Dr. Fritz about the patient who had shared a room with Nina.*Well, well.* Sam pondered. *How convenient is this? All the people I need to see, all under one roof. It's like a compact information center for criminal investigation. Welcome to* Corruption Mall!

As was the protocol, Nurse Marx knocked three times and opened the door. Lieutenant Werner was just getting up to leave and did not seem at all surprised to see the nurse, but he recognized Sam from the news van. A question brushed on Werner's brow, but Nurse Marx stopped and lost all the color in her face.

"Marlene?" Werner asked with an inquisitive look. "What is it, baby?"

She stood motionless, in awe, while slowly a twinge of terror overwhelmed her. Her eyes read the nametag on Dr. Fritz's white coat, but she shook her head in a daze. Werner came to her and cradled her face as she prepared to scream. Sam knew something was up, but as he knew none of these people, it was vague at best.

"Marlene!" Werner shouted to jerk her to her senses. Marlene Marx allowed her voice to return and she roared at the man in the coat. "You're not Dr. Fritz! You are not Dr. Fritz!"

Before Werner could fully grasp what was happening, the imposter propelled forward and grabbed Werner's gun from his shoulder holster. But Sam was quicker in his reaction and he lunged ahead to push Werner out of the way, thwarting the malformed attacker's attempt to arm himself. Nurse Marx retreated from the office, hysterically crying for security to help.

Narrowing his eyes through the plate glass window in the double doors of the ward, one of the officers Nurse Marx had previously summoned tried to distinguish the shape running toward him and his colleague.

"Heads up, Klaus," he scoffed to his colleague, "Polly Paranoid is back."

"Good God, but she is really moving, huh?" the other officer noted.

"She is crying wolf again. Look, it's not like we get a whole lot of action on this shift or anything, but being fucked with is not what I see as keeping busy, you know?" the first officer replied.

"Nurse Marx!" the second officer exclaimed. "Who can we threaten for you now?"

Marlene dove at speed, landing right in his arms, clawing at him.

"Dr. Fritz's office! Go! Go, for God's sake!" she screamed as people started to stare.

When Nurse Marx started tugging at the man's sleeve, pulling him along with her towards the office of Dr. Fritz, the officers realized that this time it was not a hunch. Again, they raced towards the distant hallway just out of their sight as the nurse cried for them to catch what she kept calling *the monster.* Confused as they were, they followed the sound of the altercation ahead and soon discovered why the frantic, young nurse referred to the imposter as a monster.

Sam Cleave was busy exchanging blows with the old man, stepping in his way every time he went for the door. Werner was sitting on the floor, dazed and surrounded by shards of glass and a few kidney dishes that had gone sprawling after the impostor had knocked him out cold with a bedpan and toppled the small cabinet where Dr. Fritz kept his Petri dishes and other breakables.

"Mother of God, look at that thing!" the one officer yelled at his partner as they elected to bring the seemingly invincible culprit down by piling their bodies onto him. Sam struggled out of the way as the two officers subdued the offender in the white coat. Sam's brow was decorated in crimson ribbons that elegantly lined the features of his cheekbone. Next to him, Werner was holding the back of his skull where the bedpan had connected painfully.

"I think I'm going to need stitches," Werner told Nurse Marx as she carefully crept around the doorway into the office. His dark hair sported bloody clumps where the gash smiled. Sam watched how the officers restrained the odd-looking man with threats of deadly force until he had finally yielded. The other two loiterers Sam had seen with Werner outside the news van showed up too.

"Hey, what's the tourist doing here?" Kohl asked when he saw Sam.

"He's not a tourist," Nurse Marx defended as she held Werner's head. "This is a world renowned journalist!"

"Really?" Kohl asked sincerely. "Nice." And he held out his hand to pull Sam to his feet. Himmelfarb just shook his head, standing back to give everyone room to move. The officers cuffed the man, but they'd been informed that the Air Force representatives had jurisdiction in this case.

"We must hand him over to you, I believe," the officer conceded to Werner and his men. "Let us just finalize our paperwork so that he can be officially transferred into military custody."

"Thank you, officer. Just sort it all out right here in the office. We do not need the public and the patients to get alarmed all over again," Werner advised.

The police and security guards took the man aside while Nurse Marx performed her duty even against her own will, dressing the old man's cuts and abrasions. She was certain eerie face could easily haunt the dreams of the most hardened of men. It was not that he was ugly, per se, but his lack of features made him ugly. In her gut she felt a strange sense of pity mingle with her repugnance as she dabbed his scarcely bleeding scratches with an alcohol swab.

His eyes were perfectly shaped, if not rather attractive in their exotic nature. However it appeared as though the rest of his face had been sacrificed for their quality. His skull was uneven and his nose seemed almost non-existent. But it was his mouth that struck a nerve with Marlene.

"You suffer from Microstomia," she remarked to him.

"Systemic sclerosis in a minor form, yes, causing small mouth phenomenon," he replied casually, as if he were there to get a blood test. His words were well pronounced, nonetheless, and his German accent was virtually flawless by now.

"Any prior treatment?" she asked. It was a stupid question, but if she did not engage in medical small talk with him he would repulse her so much more. Being in conversation with him was much the same as speaking to Sam the patient when he had been there – an intelligent conversation with a cogent monster.

"No," was all he answered, deleting his capacity for sarcasm only because she had cared to ask. His tone was innocent, as if he were fully accepting her medical scrutiny while the men babbled in the background.

"What is your name, pal?" the one officer asked him loudly.

"Marduk. Peter Marduk," he answered.

"You're not German?" Werner asked. "Geez, you had me fooled."

Marduk wished he could smile in response to the ill-formed compliment on his German, but the tightening of the tissue around his mouth refused him the privilege.

"Identity documents," the officer snapped, still nursing his swollen lip from a stray punch during the arrest. Marduk slowly slipped his hand into his jacket pocket under Dr. Fritz's white coat. "I need to take his statement for our records, Lieutenant."

Werner nodded approvingly. They were authorized to track down and kill Löwenhagen, not to apprehend an old man who impersonated a doctor. Yet now that Werner had been told why Schmidt was really after Löwenhagen, they could benefit well from more information from Marduk.

"So Dr. Fritz is dead too, then?" Nurse Marx asked softly when she leaned in to cover a particularly deep cut from the steel links of Sam Cleave's watch.

"No."

Her heart jumped. "What do you mean? If you were pretending to be him in his office you had to have killed him first."

"This is not the tale of the annoying little girl with the red shawl and her grandmother, my dear," the old man sighed. "Unless it is the version where the grandmother is still alive in the wolf's belly."

19

—————

THE BABEL EXPOSITION

"We found him! He's fine. Just knocked out and gagged!" one of the police officers announced when they found Dr. Fritz. He was exactly where Marduk had told them to look. They could not hold Marduk without concrete proof that he'd committed the murders of the precious nights, so Marduk had yielded up his location.

The imposter insisted that he'd only overpowered the doctor and assumed his guise to allow him to exit the hospital without suspicion. But Werner's appointment had blindsided him, forcing him to play the role a little longer, "...until Nurse Marx spoiled my plans," he lamented, shrugging in defeat.

A few minutes after the police captain in charge of the Karlsruhe Police headquarters showed up, Marduk's brief statement was completed. They could only charge him for petty offenses like minor assault.

"Lieutenant, after the police are finished I must clear the

detainee medically before you take him," Nurse Marx told Werner in front of the officers. "It is hospital protocol. Otherwise the Luftwaffe might incur legal consequences."

No sooner had she touched on the subject when it became relevant in the flesh. A woman walked into the office, a posh leather briefcase in her hand and dressed in corporate attire. "Good day," she addressed the police officers with a firm, but cordial tone. "Miriam Inkley, British legal liaison of the W.U.O. branch in Germany. I understand that this sensitive matter has been brought to your attention, Captain?"

The police commander concurred with the lawyer. "Yes, it has, madam. However, we are still sitting with an open homicide case and the military is claiming our only suspect. That presents a problem."

"Not to worry, Captain. Come, let us discuss the joint operations of the Air Force Criminal Investigation Unit and the Karlsruhe Police HQ in another room," the mature British woman offered. "You can authorize the details if they satisfy your investigation in association with the W.U.O. If not, we can arrange a future meeting to better accommodate your grievances."

"No, please, let me see what the W.U.O. has in mind. As long as we bring the guilty individual to justice. I don't care about the media coverage, just justice for the families of these three victims," the police captain was heard saying as the two of them walked off into the corridor. The officers said goodbye and followed, paperwork in hand.

"So the W.U.O. even knows that the pilot was involved in some underhanded PR stunt?" Nurse Marx worried. "That is pretty serious. I hope this does not foil the big treaty they're going to sign soon."

"No, the W.U.O. does not know anything about this," Sam said. He was wrapping his bleeding knuckles in a sterile bandage. "In fact, we're the only ones who are privy to the escaped pilot and, hopefully soon, the reasons for his pursuit." Sam looked at Marduk who nodded in compliance.

"But..." Marlene Marx tried to protest, pointing at the now empty door where the British lawyer had just told them otherwise.

"Her name is Margaret. She just saved you lot a whole bucket of legal hold-ups that would have procrastinated your little hunt," Sam revealed. "She is a reporter for a Scottish newspaper."

"A friend of yours, then," Werner assumed.

"Aye," Sam confirmed. Kohl looked befuddled as always.

"Unbelievable!" Nurse Marx threw her hands up. "Is anyone who they say they are anymore? Mr. Marduk plays Dr. Fritz. And Mr. Cleave plays tourist. That reporter lady plays a W.U.O. lawyer. Nobody shows who they really are! It's just like that story in the Bible where nobody could speak each other's languages and there was all this confusion."

"Babel," came the collective answers from the men.

"Yes!" she snapped her fingers. "You're all speaking a different language and this office is the tower of Babel."

"Don't forget that you pretend that you're not romantically

involved with the Lieutenant here," Sam stopped her with a reprimanding index finger.

"How did you know?" she asked.

Sam just cocked his head, declining even bringing her attention to the closeness and petting between the two. Nurse Marx blushed when Werner winked at her.

"Then there is the bunch of you who pretend you are undercover officers when in fact you are distinguished fighter pilots of the German Luftwaffe Operational Forces, just like the prey you are hunting for God knows what reason," Sam eviscerated their deceit.

"Told you he was a brilliant investigative journalist," Marlene whispered to Werner.

"And you," said Sam, cornering the still dazed Dr. Fritz. "Where do you fit in?"

"I swear I had no idea!" Dr. Fritz confessed. "He just asked me to keep it for him. So I told him where I had put it in case I was not on duty when he was discharged! But I swear I never knew that thing could do that! My God, I almost lost my mind seeing that...that...unnatural transformation!"

Werner and his men, along with Sam and Nurse Marx, stood confounded at the doctor's incoherent babbling. Only Marduk appeared to know what was going on, but he remained quiet to watch the madness unfold in the doctor's office.

"Well, I'm thoroughly confused. How about you lads?" Sam declared with his bandaged hand at his side. They all nodded in a resounding chorus of disapproving murmurs.

"I think it is time for some exposition to help us all unmask each other's real intentions," Werner suggested. "After all, we might even be able to help each other with our various pursuits, instead of trying to fight each other."

"Wise man," Marduk chipped in.

"I have to do my last rounds," Marlene sighed. "If I don't show, Sister Barken will know something is up. Will you fill me in tomorrow, darling?"

"I will," Werner fibbed. He then kissed her goodbye before she opened the door. She looked back at the admittedly fascinating anomaly that was Peter Marduk and blessed the old man with a kind smile.

When the door closed, a thick atmosphere of testosterone and distrust overwhelmed the occupants of Dr. Fritz's office. There was not only one Alpha here, but each man knew something the other lacked knowledge of. Sam started eventually.

"Let us make this snappy, shall we? I have a very urgent concern to attend to after this. Dr. Fritz, I need you to send Dr. Nina Gould's test results to Mannheim before we sort out whatever you have sinned," Sam ordered the doctor.

"Nina? Dr. Nina Gould is alive?" he asked in awe, letting out a sigh of relief and crossing himself like the good Catholic he was. "That is wonderful news!"

"Small woman? Dark hair and eyes like hellfire?" Marduk asked Sam.

"Aye, that would be her, no doubt!" Sam smiled.

"I'm afraid she took my presence here wrongly too," Marduk

said, looking sorry about it. He decided not to share that he had slapped the poor girl when she had made trouble. But when he told her she would die, he'd only meant that Löwenhagen was at large and dangerous, something he did not have time to explain all over now.

"That's alright. She is like a bite of hot pepper to just about everyone," Sam replied while Dr. Fritz drew Nina's hard copy folder and scanned the test results into his computer. Once the document with the awful material was scanned in, he asked Sam for the e-mail of Nina's doctor at Mannheim. Sam furnished him with a card containing all of the details and carried on clumsily putting a fabric plaster on his brow. As he winced, he cast a glance toward Marduk, the man responsible for the cut, but the old man pretended not to see.

"There," Dr. Fritz exhaled long and hard, relieved that his patient was still alive. "I'm just elated that she is alive. How she got out of here with that poor eyesight, I'll never know."

"Your pal led her all the way out, doctor," Marduk enlightened him. "You know, the young bastard you gave the mask to so that he could wear the faces of the people he killed in the name of greed?"

"I did – not – know!" Dr. Fritz seethed, still sour at the old man for the throbbing headache he was suffering.

"Hey, hey!" Werner stopped the ensuing argument. "We're here to resolve this, not fuck it up even more! Now, first I want to know what *your*," he pointed straight at Marduk, "involvement with Löwenhagen is. We were sent to apprehend him and that is all we know. Then, when I interviewed you, all this mask business came out."

"As I told you before, I do not know who Löwenhagen is," Marduk insisted.

"The pilot who crashed the plane is Olaf Löwenhagen," Himmelfarb replied. "He burned in the crash, but somehow survived and made it to the hospital."

There was a long pause. Everyone waited for Marduk to explain why he was chasing after Löwenhagen in the first place. The old man knew that, if he told them why he was pursuing the young man, he would have to reveal why he had set him alight too. Marduk took a deep breath and started shedding some light on the crow's nest of misunderstanding.

"I was under the impression that the man I pursued from the blazing fuselage of the Tornado fighter plane was a pilot named Neumand," he said.

"Neumand? That can't be. Neumand is on leave, probably gambling away the last of his family's coins in some back alley," Himmelfarb scoffed. Kohl and Werner nodded approvingly.

"Well, I chased him from the scene of the crash. I pursued him because he had the mask. When I saw the mask I had to exterminate him. He was a thief, a common thief, I tell you! And what he stole was too powerful for any foolish imbecile like that to handle! So I had to stop him the only way a Masker can be stopped," Marduk said anxiously.

"A *Masker*?" Kohl asked. "Man, that sounds like a horror movie villain." He smiled, patting Himmelfarb on the shoulder.

"Grow up," Himmelfarb grunted.

"A Masker is one who assumes the face of another by using the Babylonian Mask. It's the mask your evil friend made away with along with Dr. Gould," Marduk explained, but they could all see that he was reluctant to clarify more.

"Go on," Sam sniffed, hoping that his guess as to the rest of the description would be incorrect. "How does one kill a Masker?"

"By fire," Marduk replied, almost too quickly. Sam could see that he just wanted to get it off his chest. "Look, to the modern world this is all old wives' tales. I don't expect any of you to understand."

"Never mind that," Werner dismissed the angst. "I want to know how this is possible, to put on a mask and have your face change into someone else's. What part of that is even rational?"

"Believe me, Lieutenant. I have seen things people only read in mythology, so I would not be so quick as to deem this irrational," Sam declared. "Most of the absurdities I once scoffed at I've since found to be in some way scientifically plausible, once you dust off the embellishments of ages added to make something practical sound ridiculously fabricated."

Marduk nodded, grateful that someone there had the capacity to at least hear him out. His sharp look jumped between the men who listened to him as he studied their expressions, wondering if he should even bother.

But he had to bother because his prey had escaped him for the most nefarious undertaking of recent years – to ignite World War III.

THE INCREDIBLE TRUTH

·

*D*r. Fritz had kept quiet all this time, but at this point he felt he had to add something to the conversation. With his eyes cast down to the hand in his lap, he testified as to the strangeness of the mask. "When that patient came in, burning, he asked that I keep the mask for him. At first I thought nothing of it, you know? I thought it was precious to him and that it was probably the one thing he had saved from a house fire or something."

He looked up at them, perplexed and horrified. Then he locked onto Marduk, as if he felt the need to make the old man understand why he'd pretended not see what he saw.

"At one point, after I put the thing down, uh, on its face, so to speak, so that I could attend to my patient. Some of the dead flesh that had peeled off his shoulder clung to my glove; I had to shake it off to continue working." He was now taking shivering breaths. "But some of it landed inside the mask and I swear to God..."

Dr. Fritz shook his head, too embarrassed to recount the nightmarish and ludicrous claim.

"Tell them! Tell them, in the name of the holy! They have to know that I am not insane!" the old man cried. His words were troubled and slow, for the shape of his mouth made speech difficult, but his voice penetrated the ears of everyone present like a crack of thunder.

"I have to finish my work. I'm still on the clock, I'll have you know," Dr. Fritz tried to change the subject, but nobody moved a muscle to support him. Dr. Fritz's brow quivered as he reconsidered.

"When...when the flesh fell into the mask," he continued, "the surface of the mask...took shape?" Dr. Fritz found that he could not believe his own words, yet he remembered what had happened just so! The faces of the three pilots remained frozen in disbelief. Sam Cleave and Marduk, however, had not an inkling of judgment or surprise on their faces. "The inside of the mask became...a face, just," he inhaled deeply, "just concavely. I told myself that it was the long hours and the shape of the mask playing tricks on me, but once the bloody tissue was wiped from it the face disappeared."

Nobody said anything. Some of the men had a hard time believing it, while the others tried to formulate possible ways in which this could have occurred. Marduk thought this would be a good time to append the doctor's stunner with more of the incredible, but this time to present it more from scientific standpoint. "That is how it happens. A rather macabre method is employed by the Babylonian Mask, utilizing dead human tissue to absorb the genetic material contained therein and then forming that individual's face as the mask's."

"Jesus!" Werner said. He watched Himmelfarb run past him, headed for the en suite toilet. "Yes, I don't blame you, Corporal."

"Gentlemen, may I remind you I have a ward to run." Dr. Fritz reiterated his previous statement.

"There is...more," Marduk jumped in with a slow, boney hand aloft to accentuate his point.

"Oh great," Sam smiled sarcastically, clearing his throat.

Marduk paid him no attention and laid out more unwritten rules. "Once the Masker takes on the facial features of the donor, the mask can only be removed by fire. Only fire can dislodge it from the Masker's own face." He then added solemnly, "and that is why I had to do what I did."

Himmelfarb could take no more. "I am a pilot, for God's sake. This mumbo-jumbo shit is definitely not for me. This is all too Hannibal Lecter for me. I'm out, friends."

"You were given a mission, Himmelfarb," said Werner sternly, but the Corporal of the Schleswig Air Base was out no matter what the cost.

"I am aware of that, Lieutenant!" he shouted. "And I will be sure to convey my grievance to our esteemed commander myself, so that you will not be reprimanded for my behavior." He sighed, wiping his moist, pale brow. "I'm sorry, guys, but I cannot handle this. Good luck, really. Call me when you need an airman. That is all I am." He left and closed the door behind him.

"Cheers, lad," Sam bade goodbye. He then addressed Marduk with the one vexatious question that had been hounding him since the phenomenon was first explained. "Marduk, I'm having trouble with something here. Tell me what happens if a person just puts on the mask without any dead flesh action?"

"Nothing."

One cohesive chorus of disappointment ensued among the others. They had expected more far-fetched rules of the game, Marduk realized, but he was not about to make things up for entertainment. He just shrugged.

"Nothing happens?" Kohl marveled. "You don't die an excruciating death or asphyxiate to death? You put on the mask and *nothing* happens."

"Nothing happens, son. It is just a mask. Which is why very few people know about its sinister power," Marduk replied.

"What a boner killer," Kohl complained.

"Alright, so if you wear the mask and your face becomes someone else's – and you don't get set on fire by a crazy old bastard like you – do you have the other person's face forever?" Werner asked.

"Ah, good one!" Sam exclaimed, immersed in fascination for it all. If he were an amateur he would be chewing the end of his Biro and taking notes like mad by now, but Sam was a veteran journalist able to memorize countless facts as he listened. That, and he was secretly recording the whole conversation from the tape recorder in his pocket.

"You go blind," Marduk answered nonchalantly. "Then you become like a mad animal and die."

Again, a hiss of amazement coursed through them. Then a chuckle or two ensued. One was from Dr. Fritz. By now he had realized that trying to throw the bunch out was futile and besides, he was becoming interested now.

"Wow, Mr. Marduk, you just seem to have a ready answer for everything, don't you?" Dr. Fritz shook his head with an amused smirk.

"Yes, I do, my dear doctor," Marduk agreed. "I am almost eighty years old and have been responsible for this and other relics since I was a fifteen-year-old boy. By now I have not only familiarized myself with the rules, but regrettably seen them in action too many times."

Dr. Fritz suddenly felt foolish for his arrogance and his face showed it. "My apologies."

"I understand, Dr. Fritz. Men are always quick to dismiss what they cannot control as lunacy. But when it comes to their own absurd practices and idiotic courses of action they can throw almost any explanation at you to justify it," the old man said with difficulty.

The doctor could see that the restricted muscle tissue around his mouth was making it really uncomfortable for the man to continue speaking.

"Um, is there any reason why people who keep the mask on go blind and lose their minds?" Kohl asked his first sincere question.

"That part has remained mainly lore and myth, son," Marduk shrugged. "I've seen it happen only a few times over the years. Most people who've used the mask for insidious purposes had no idea what would happen to them after they got their vengeance. Like every evil drive or desire attained, there is a price. But mankind never learns. Power is for gods. Humility is for men."

Werner had been calculating it all in his head. "Let me recap," he said. "If you wear the mask as just a mask, it is harmless and useless."

"Yes," replied Marduk, sinking his chin and blinking slowly.

"And if you peel some skin off some dead target and put it on the inside of the mask and then put it on your face...God, I gag just saying that...your face becomes that person's face, right?"

"Another Brownie for Team Werner." Sam smiled, and pointed when Marduk nodded.

"But then you have to burn it off with fire or wear it and go blind before going crazy eventually," Werner frowned, concentrating to get his ducks in a row.

"Correct," Marduk affirmed.

Dr. Fritz had one more query. "Has anyone ever figured out how to escape any of these fates, Mr. Marduk? Has anyone ever liberated the mask without blindness or a fiery demise?"

"Like Löwenhagen did? He actually put it back on again to take Dr. Hilt's face and leave the hospital! How did he do that?" asked Sam.

"The fire dislodged it the first time, Sam. He was only fortunate enough to survive. The skin is the only way to evade the fate of the Babylonian Mask," Marduk said, sounding utterly indifferent. It had become so much a part of his existence that he had grown tired of reciting the same old facts.

"The...the *skin*?" Sam cringed.

"That is exactly what it is. It is essentially the *skin* of the Babylonian Mask. It must be applied to the face of the Masker in time, to dissemble the fusion of the Masker's face and the mask. But our poor, disillusioned quarry has no idea of this. He will soon realize his mistake, if he has not already," Marduk answered. "The blindness usually takes no more than three or four days, so wherever he is, I hope he isn't driving."

"Would serve him right. Fucker!" Kohl grimaced.

"Couldn't agree more," Dr. Fritz said. "But gentlemen, I really do have to implore you to leave before the administrative staff catches wind of our overdrawn pleasantries here."

To Dr. Fritz's relief they all agreed this time. They retrieved their coats and slowly prepared to leave the office. With nods of acknowledgement and final words of parting the Air Force pilots left, keeping Marduk in their custody for show. They elected to meet up with Sam a bit later. With this new turn of events and the much needed sorting out of confusing facts, they wanted to rethink their roles in the big scheme of things.

Sam and Margaret met up in her hotel restaurant while Marduk and the two pilots were on their way to the Air Base to report to Schmidt. Now Werner knew that Marduk was familiar with his commander as per their earlier interview, yet he did not yet know why Schmidt would keep knowledge of the sinister mask to himself. Granted, it was a priceless artifact, but with his position in a pivotal body such as the German Luftwaffe, Werner figured there must be a more politically motivated reason behind Schmidt's hunt for the Babylonian Mask.

"What will you tell your commander about me?" Marduk asked the two young men he accompanied as they walked toward Werner's Jeep.

"I'm not sure we should tell him about you at all. From what I'm deducing here, it would be better if you help us find Löwenhagen and keep your presence a secret, Mr. Marduk. The less Captain Schmidt knows about you and your involvement, the better," Werner said.

"I'll see you at the base!" Kohl hollered from four cars away, unlocking his own car.

Werner nodded. "Remember, Marduk doesn't exist and we could not yet find Löwenhagen, right?"

"Got it!" Kohl approved the plan with a small salute and a boyish grin. He got in his car and drove off as the late afternoon light set the skyline of the town ablaze ahead of him. It was almost sundown and they had reached the second day of their search, still ending the day without success.

"I suppose we're going to have to start looking for blind airmen?" Werner asked quite sincerely, regardless of how ridiculous his request sounded. "It's the third day since Löwenhagen used the mask to escape the hospital, so he should be having trouble with his eyes by now."

"That is correct," Marduk replied. "If his system is strong, which it is not thanks to the fire bath I gave him, he could take longer to lose his sight. This is why the West did not understand the old ways of Mesopotamia and Babylonia and deemed us all heretics and murderous brutes. When ancient kings and chieftains burned the blind in witch-like executions, it was not out of cruelty of false accusation. Most of those instances were the direct cause of employing the Babylonian Mask for their own subterfuge."

"*Most* of those instances?" Werner asked with a raised eyebrow as he turned the Jeep's ignition, looking suspicious of the aforementioned methods.

Marduk shrugged, "Well, everyone makes mistakes, son. Better safe than sorry."

21

THE MYSTERY OF NEUMAND AND LÖWENHAGEN

*E*xhausted and filling with a steadily growing sense of regret, Olaf Löwenhagen sat down in a pub near Darmstadt. It had been two days since he'd deserted Nina at Frau Bauer's house, but he could not afford to lug a partner along on such a covert assignment; especially one that had to be led around like a mule. He was hoping to use Dr. Hilt's money to buy a meal. He also contemplated getting rid of his cell phone, just in case it was being traced. By now the authorities had to have realized that he was the one responsible for the murders at the hospital, which is why he did not commandeer Hilt's vehicle to make his way to Captain Schmidt, who was at Schleswig Air Base at the time.

He decided to risk using Hilt's cell phone to make one call. This would probably land him in hot water with Schmidt as cell phone calls could be traced, but he had no other choice. With his safety compromised and his mission gone dreadfully wrong, he had to resort to more hazardous avenues of communication to establish a connection with the man who had sent him on the mission in the first place.

"Another Pilsner, sir?" the waiter asked suddenly, jolting Löwenhagen's heart into overdrive. He looked up at the dim-witted waiter with a voice of deep boredom.

"Yes, thank you." He changed his mind quickly. "Wait, no. I'll have schnapps please. And something to eat."

"You have to take something from the menu, sir. Anything you like there?" the waiter asked indifferently.

"Just bring me a seafood dish," Löwenhagen sighed, vexed.

The waiter scoffed and smirked, "Sir, as you can see we don't offer seafood. Please order a dish we actually offer."

Had Löwenhagen not been waiting for an important meeting or had he not been weak from hunger, he may well have used the privilege of wearing Hilt's face to bash in the skull of the sarcastic cretin. "Just bring me a steak, then. Geeeezusss! Just, I don't know, surprise me!" the airman yelled furiously.

"Yes, sir," the stunned waiter replied, gathering up the menu and beer glass rapidly.

"And don't forget the schnapps first!" he shouted after the apron-donning idiot, who scampered towards the kitchen through the tables of staring patrons. Löwenhagen sneered at them and emitted what sounded like a low growl that crawled out from deep in his gullet. Disturbed by the dangerous looking man, some people left the establishment while the others carried on with nervous conversations.

An attractive young waitress dared to bring him his drink as a favor to her terrified colleague. (The waiter was collecting himself in the kitchen, preparing to face the irate customer once his food was ready.) She smiled apprehensively as she set down the glass and announced, "Schnapps for you, sir."

"Thank you," was all he said, to her surprise.

Löwenhagen, twenty-seven years of age, sat contemplating his future in the cozy lighting of the pub as the sun abandoned the day outside, painting the windows in darkness. The music grew a bit louder as the evening crowd dribbled in like a reluctant leak in a ceiling. While he waited for his food, he ordered five more stiff drinks and as the soothing hell of alcohol burned inside his injured flesh he thought of how he had come to this point.

Never in his life did he think that he would become a cold-blooded killer, a killer for profit no less, and at such a tender age. Most men devolved as they aged, becoming heartless swine for the promise of monetary gain. Not him. He had been aware as a fighter pilot that he would have to kill scores of people in combat someday, but that would be for his country.

Defending Germany and the W.U.O.'s utopian goals for the new world was his first and foremost duty and desire. Taking lives for this purpose was par for the course, yet now he was engaging in a murderous spree to serve the wishes of a Luftwaffe commander that had nothing to do with Germany's freedom or the world's well-being. In fact, he was now accomplishing the contrary. It depressed him almost as much as his dwindling eye sight and increasingly challenging temperament.

What bothered him most was the way in which Neumand had screamed when Löwenhagen set him on fire the first time. Captain Schmidt had hired Löwenhagen in what the commander had called an extremely covert operation. It had followed the recent deployment of their squadron just outside the city of Mosul, Iraq.

From what the commander had told Löwenhagen in confidence, Flieger Neumand had been sent by Schmidt to procure an obscure and ancient relic from a private collection while they were stationed in Iraq during the last plague of bombings aimed at the W.U.O. and especially the C.I.T.E. branch there. Neumand, once a teenage offender, had the skill set needed to break into the home of the wealthy collector and steal the Babylonian Mask.

He was given a picture of the slim, skull-like relic and with that he managed to steal the thing from the brass box it slept in. Soon after his successful plunder, Neumand returned to Germany with the prize he'd attained for Schmidt, but Schmidt did not count on the weaknesses of the men he chose to do his dirty work. Neumand was a compulsive gambler. On his first night back he took the mask with him to one of his favorite gambling haunts, a back alley dive in Dillenburg.

Not only did he commit the most reckless of practices by carrying an invaluable, *stolen* artifact around with him, but he invoked the rage of Captain Schmidt by not delivering the mask as discreetly and urgently as he'd been hired to do. On learning that the squadron had returned and finding Neumand absent, Schmidt immediately contacted a fickle outcast from his previous Air Base barracks to acquire the relic from Neumand by any means necessary.

As he sat thinking about that night, Löwenhagen felt his seething hate for Captain Schmidt spread throughout his mind. He was the cause of unnecessary casualties. He was the cause of greed-fuelled injustice. He was the reason Löwenhagen would never have his attractive features back again, and that was by far the most unforgivable crime the commander's avarice had imposed upon Löwenhagen's life – what was left of it.

Hilt was handsome enough but for Löwenhagen, having lost his individuality struck deeper than any physical mutilation ever could. To add to it, his eyes had begun to fail him to such an extent that he could not even read the menu to order his food. The humiliation was almost worse than the discomfort and physical handicap. He swigged his schnapps and clicked his fingers above his head for another.

In his head he could hear a thousand voices passing the buck to everyone else for his ill-fated choices and his own inner reason being left mute at how fast things had gone wrong. He recalled the night he had procured the mask, and how Neumand had refused to relinquish his hard earned loot. He'd followed Neumand's trail to the gambling den under the stairs of a nightclub. There he'd bided his time, posing as just another party animal frequenting the site.

By just after one in the morning Neumand had gambled away everything and he was now in a double or nothing challenge.

"I'll float you €1000 if you let me keep that mask as a surety," Löwenhagen offered.

"Are you kidding?" Neumand cackled in his drunken state. "This fucking thing is worth a million times that!" He'd held up the mask for all to see, but thankfully his inebriated state made the shady company he was in doubt his sincerity on the item. Löwenhagen could not allow them to think twice about it, so he acted quickly.

"Right then, I'll play you for the stupid mask. At least I can get your ass back to the base." He'd said this especially loud, hoping to convince the others that he was just trying to get the mask to get his friend to go home. It was a good thing Löwenhagen's deceptive past had honed his skills of guile. He was extremely convincing when he ran a con, a trait that usually benefited him. Until now, when it had ultimately caused him his future.

The mask sat in the middle of the round table, surrounded by three men. Löwenhagen could hardly object when another gambler wanted in on the action. The man was a local biker, a mere foot soldier in his chapter, but it would have been suspicious to deny him access to a poker game in a public dump known to local low lives everywhere.

Even with his cheating skills, Löwenhagen found that he could not swindle the mask from the stranger sporting the black and white the Gremium emblem on his leather cut-off.

"Black seven rules, motherfuckers!" the big biker bellowed when Löwenhagen folded and Neumand's hand yielded an impotent three-of-a-kind of jacks. Neumand was too drunk to make an effort to get back the mask, although he was clearly devastated by the loss.

"Oh Jesus! Oh sweet Jesus, he is going to kill me! He is going to kill me!" was all Neumand could utter with his hands cradling his bowed head. He sat there moaning until the next group who wanted the table told him to piss off or end up in the pot. Neumand walked away, mumbling to himself like a lunatic, but again it was written off as a drunken stupor and those he shouldered out of his way took it just that way. Löwenhagen followed Neumand, having no idea of the esoteric nature of the relic the biker was swinging in his hand somewhere ahead. The biker stopped for a while, bragging to a bunch of girls that the skull mask was going to look wicked under his German army styled piss pot helmet. Soon he realized that Neumand was, in fact, following the biker into a shadowy concrete pit where a row of motorcycles gleamed in the pale rays of the lights that did not quite reach to the parking area.

Quietly he watched as Neumand pulled out his gun, stepped out of the shadows and shot the biker point blank in the face. Gunshots were not exactly an oddity around these parts of town, although some people alerted the other bikers. Their silhouettes rose over the edge of the parking pit soon after, but they were still too far away to see what had happened.

Choking for what he beheld, Löwenhagen played witness to the gruesome ritual of slicing off a piece of the dead man's flesh with his own knife. Neumand dropped the bleeding tissue into the underside of the mask and started stripping his victim as hastily as he could manage with his drunken fingers. Wide-eyed and shocked, Löwenhagen learned the secret of the Babylonian Mask there and then. Now he knew why Schmidt was so eager to get his hands on it.

With his new grotesque looks, Neumand rolled the body off into the trashcans a few meters away from the last vehicle in the dark and then nonchalantly climbed onto the man's motorcycle. Four days later, Neumand took back the mask and absconded. Löwenhagen tracked him down outside the

Schleswig base, where he was hiding from Schmidt's wrath. Neumand still rocked the biker look, complete with shades and dirty jeans, but he had gotten rid of the club colors and the bike. Mannheim's chapter of Gremium was looking for the impostor and it wasn't worth the risk. When Neumand encountered Löwenhagen he had laughed like a madman, rambling on incoherently in what sounded like an ancient Arabic dialect.

Then he lifted the knife and tried to cut off his own face.

22

***

BLIND GOD RISING

"So, you finally made contact." A voice ripped through Löwenhagen's body from behind his left shoulder. He instantly pictured the Devil, and he was not far off.

"Captain Schmidt," he acknowledged, but did not rise nor salute, for obvious reasons. "You will excuse me for not responding in proper fashion. I am, after all, wearing another man's face, you see."

"Absolutely. Jack Daniels, please," Schmidt told the waiter before he'd even reached the table with Löwenhagen's food.

"Put the plate down first, pal!" Löwenhagen shouted, prompting the confused man to obey. The manager of the restaurant was standing nearby, waiting for just one more transgression before asking the abusive man to leave.

"Now, I see you have found out what the mask does," murmured Schmidt under his breath and dropping his head to check for eavesdroppers.

"I saw what it did the night your little bitch Neumand used it to make away with it—," Löwenhagen said in a low tone, barely breathing in between bites as he wolfed down the first half of his meat like an animal.

"So what do you propose to do now? Blackmail me for money like Neumand was doing?" asked Schmidt, playing for time. He was very aware of what the relic took from those who used it.

"Blackmail you?" Löwenhagen shrieked with a mouthful of pink meat minced between his teeth. "Are you fucking kidding me? I want it off, Captain. You are going to get a surgeon to take it off."

"Why? I recently heard you were burned pretty badly. I would have thought that you would want to keep the face of a dashing doctor instead of a melted mess of flesh where your face once was," the commander replied evilly. He watched amusedly as Löwenhagen struggled to cut his steak, straining his failing eyes to find the edges.

"Fuck you!" cursed Löwenhagen. He could not see Schmidt's face very well, but he felt an overwhelming urge to plunge the steak knife into the general vicinity of his eyes and hope for the best. "I want it off before I turn into a bat shit crazy...r-rabid...fucking..."

"Is that what happened to Neumand?" interrupted Schmidt, helping with the sentence structure of the toiling young man. "What exactly happened, Löwenhagen? By the gambling fetish that imbecile had I can understand his motive for keeping what is rightfully mine. What perplexes me, though, is why you would want to keep it from me this long before contacting me."

"I was going to give it to you the day after I took it from Neumand, but I found myself on fire that very same night, my dear captain." Löwenhagen was now stuffing chunks of meat in his mouth by hand. Horrified, the people directly around them began staring and whispering.

"Excuse me, gentlemen," the manager said tactfully in a hushed tone.

But Löwenhagen was too intolerant to listen. He tossed a black American Express card on the table and said, "Listen, bring us a bottle of tequila and I'll buy all these curious assholes a round if they stop looking at me like that!"

Some of his sympathizers at the pool table cheered. The rest of the people went back to their business.

"Don't worry, we'll be leaving soon. Just get everyone their drinks and let my friend here finish his food, okay?" Schmidt excused their present state with his *holier than thou*, civilized manner. It won the manager's disinterest for a few more minutes.

"Now tell me how it was that you ended up with my mask in a goddamn public institution where anyone could have taken it," Schmidt whispered. The bottle of tequila arrived and he poured two shot glasses.

Löwenhagen swallowed with great difficulty. The alcohol had obviously not doused the agony of his internal injuries effectively, but he was ravenous. He told the commander what had happened mostly to save face, not to make excuses. The entire scenario that he'd been fuming about earlier replayed itself as he told Schmidt everything that had led up to where he'd found Neumand speaking in tongues in the biker's guise.

"Arabic? That is unsettling," admitted Schmidt. "What you heard was actually *Akkadian*? Amazing!"

"Who gives a shit?" Löwenhagen barked.

"Then? How did you get the mask from him?" Schmidt asked, almost smiling at the interesting facts of the story.

"I had no idea how to get the mask back. I mean, here he was with a fully developed face and no trace of the mask that was hiding under it. My God, listen to what I'm saying! This is all nightmarish and surreal!"

"Carry on," Schmidt urged.

"I asked him straight up how I can help him get the mask off, you know? But he...he..." Löwenhagen laughed like a rowdy drunk at the absurdity of his own words. "Captain, he bit me! Like a fucking stray dog the bastard growled as I came nearer and while I was still talking the fucker bit me on my shoulder. He took a whole chunk out! Christ! What was I supposed to think? I just starting beating him with the first piece of metal pipe I could find lying around."

"So, what did he do? Was he still speaking in Akkadian?" asked the commander, pouring another round for the two of them.

"He took off running, so I chased after him, of course. We ended up going through the east side of Schleswig, there where only we know to get in?" he told Schmidt, who nodded in turn, "Yes, I know the place, behind the auxiliary building hangar."

"That's right. We ran through there, Captain, like bats out of hell. I mean, I was ready to kill him. I was hurting badly, bleeding, fed-up with him eluding me for so long. I swear I was ready to just break his fucking head into pieces to get that mask back, you know?" growled Löwenhagen softly, sounding delightfully psychotic.

"Yes, yes. Carry on." Schmidt was pushing to hear the end of the story before his subordinate finally succumbed to the pressing insanity.

As his plate grew messier and emptier Löwenhagen spoke faster, his consonants more pronounced. "I did not know what he was trying to do, but maybe he knew how to get the mask off or something. I pursued him right into the hangar and then we were alone. I could hear the guards shouting outside the hangar. I doubt they recognized Neumand now that he had someone else's face, right?"

"Is that when he took the fighter plane?" Schmidt asked. "Was that why the plane crashed?"

Löwenhagen's eyes were almost completely blind by now, but he could still tell where shadows and solids were. A yellow tinge stained his irises, the color of a lion's eyes, but he recounted on, pinning Schmidt with his blind eyes as he lowered his voice and dipped his head a little. "My God, Captain Schmidt, how he hated *you*."

Narcissism prevented Schmidt from caring about the sentiment of Löwenhagen's declaration, but common sense had him feeling a bit tarnished – right where his soul was supposed to jitter. "Of course he did," he told his blind underling. "I'm the one who introduced him to the mask. But he was never supposed to know what it did, let alone use it for himself. The fool brought this on himself. Just like you did."

"I..." Löwenhagen lunged forward wrathfully amongst

clanging utensils and toppling glasses, "only used it to get your precious bloody relic out of the hospital and to you, you ungrateful subspecies!"

Schmidt knew Löwenhagen had served his purpose and his insubordination was of little concern anymore. He would soon expire nonetheless, so Schmidt allowed him his tantrum. "He hated you like *I* hate you! Neumand regretted ever getting involved with your evil plan to send a suicide squad into Baghdad and The Hague."

Schmidt felt his heart jump at the mention of his supposedly clandestine plan, but his face remained straight, sheltering all worry inside its steel expression.

"Spitting your name, *Schmidt*, he saluted and said he was going to visit you on a little suicide mission of your own." Löwenhagen's voice pierced through his smile. "He stood there laughing like a mad animal, screeching for relief from what he was. Still dressed like the dead biker, he went for the jet. Before I could get to him, the guards burst in. I just ran to keep from being arrested. Once outside the base, I got into my truck and raced to Büchel to try to warn you. Your cell phone was off."

"And that's when he crashed the plane outside our base," Schmidt nodded. "How am I supposed to explain the true story to Lieutenant-General Meier? He is under the impression that it was a legitimate counter-attack after what that Dutch idiot did in Iraq."

"Neumand was a first class pilot. Why he missed the target – you – is as much a pity as it is a mystery," growled Löwenhagen. Only Schmidt's silhouette still indicated his presence next to him.

"He missed because like you, my boy, he had gone blind," stated Schmidt, relishing in his victory over those who could expose him. "But you did not know about that, did you? Because Neumand wore sunglasses you did not know about his poor eyesight. Otherwise you would never have used the Babylonian Mask yourself, would you?"

"No, I would not have," grated Löwenhagen, feeling defeated to a boiling point. "But I should have known you would send someone to burn me up and get the mask back. After I drove to the crash site, I found Neumand's charred remains flung far from the fuselage. The mask had been detached from his scorched skull, so I took it to bring it back to my dear commander whom I thought I could trust." At this point his yellow eyes had gone blind. "But you already took care of that, didn't you?"

"What are you talking about?" he heard Schmidt say next to him, but he was done with the commander's deceit.

"You sent someone after me. He found me with the mask at the site of the wreckage and chased me all the way into Heidelberg until my truck ran out of fuel!" snarled Löwenhagen. "But he had enough petrol for the both of us, Schmidt. Before I could see him coming, he poured petrol all over me and set me on fire! All I could do was run to the hospital a stone's throw away, still hoping that the fire would not catch and maybe even extinguish as I ran. But no, it only got stronger and hotter, consuming my skin and my lips and my limbs until I thought I was screaming through my flesh! Do you know what it is like to feel your heart explode under the shock of smelling your own flesh burning like a steak on a grill? DO YOU?" he screamed at the captain, wearing the vicious expression of dead man.

As the manager jogged hastily to their table, Schmidt raised his hand dismissively.

"We're going. We're going. Just charge it all to that credit card," Schmidt ordered, knowing that Dr. Hilt would soon be found dead again, while his credit card statement would show that he'd lived a few days longer than initially reported.

"Come, Löwenhagen," Schmidt said urgently. "I know how we can get that mask off your face. I have no idea how to reverse the blindness, though."

He led his companion to the bar where he signed the slip. As they left, Schmidt slipped the credit card back into Löwenhagen's pocket. The staff and patrons all gave a sigh of relief. The unfortunate waiter who'd received no gratuity clicked his tongue, saying "Thank God! I hope that is the last we see of him."

23

ASSASSINATION

*M*arduk watched the clock and the small rectangle on its face with the flip-type date panels arranged to announce that it was the 28th of October. His fingers tapped on the counter while he waited for the receptionist at the Swanwasser Hotel, where Sam Cleave and his mysterious lady friend were also staying.

"There we go, Mr. Marduk. Welcome to Germany," the receptionist smiled kindly and returned Marduk's passport. Her eyes dwelled on his face for a moment too long. It made the old man wonder if it was because of his unusual face or because his identification documents stated *Iraq* as his country of origin.

"Vielen Dank," he replied. He would have smiled if he could have.

After checking into his room, he went downstairs to meet Sam and Margaret outside in the garden. They were already waiting for him when he stepped out onto the deck over-looking the swimming pool. A small, smartly dressed man had been following Marduk at a distance, but the old man was far too astute not to know.

Sam cleared his throat in a suggestive manner, but all Marduk said was "I see him."

"Of course you do," Sam said to himself, motioning to Margaret with his head. She looked up at the stranger and recoiled somewhat, but she kept it from his view. Marduk turned to look at the man following him, just enough to assess the situation. Apologetically, the man smiled and disappeared into the corridor.

"They see a passport from Iraq and they lose their bloody minds," he snapped irately as he sat down.

"Mr. Marduk, this is Margaret Crosby of the Edinburgh Post," Sam introduced them.

"Lovely to meet you, Madam," said Marduk, again using his polite nod instead of a smile.

"And you also, Mr. Marduk," Margaret replied cordially. "It's wonderful to finally meet such an informed and travelled man such as yourself." *Is she actually flirting with Marduk?* Sam wondered in amusement, as he watched the two of them shake hands.

"And how do you know this?" Marduk asked in mock surprise.

Sam lifted his recording device.

"Ah, all that business in the doctor's office is on record now." He gave the investigate journalist a stern eye.

"Not to worry, Marduk," said Sam, intending to dismiss all concern. "This is just for me and those who are going to help us track down the Babylonian Mask. As you know, Ms. Crosby here has already done her part in getting the police commander off our backs."

"Yes, some journalists have the common sense to be selective about what the world should know and...well, what the world is better off never knowing about. The Babylonian Mask and its abilities fall into the latter category. You are assured of my discretion," Margaret promised Marduk.

His image fascinated her. The British spinster had always had an affinity for the unusual and unique. He was not nearly as monstrous as the staff of Heidelberg Hospital had described him. Yes, he was clearly deformed by normal standards, but his face only added to his intriguing personality.

"That is a relief to know, Madam," he sighed.

"Please, call me Margaret," she said quickly.*Aye, some geriatric flirting going on here,* Sam decided.

"So, to the business at hand," interrupted Sam, starting into the more serious conversation. "How are we going to start looking for this Löwenhagen character?"

"I think we should discount him from the game. According to Lieutenant Werner, the man behind the procurement of the Babylonian Mask is Captain Schmidt of the German Luftwaffe. I've instructed Lieutenant Werner to go under the pretense of reporting and steal the mask from Schmidt by noon tomorrow. If I have not heard from Werner by then, we'll have to assume the worst. In that case, I myself will have to get inside the base and have a word with Schmidt. He is at the root of this whole deranged operation, and he will want to be in possession of the relic by the time the signing of the great peace treaty takes place."

"So you think he is going to impersonate the Meso-Arabian Commissioner for the signing?" asked Margaret, aptly using the new term for the Middle East since the merging of the flanking, smaller lands under one government.

"There are a million possibilities, Mada...Margaret," Marduk clarified. "He could choose to do that, but he does not speak any Arabic, so the Commissioner's people will know he is a charlatan. *Of all the times not to be able to control the minds of the masses. Imagine how easily I could have averted all of this if I still had that psychic nonsense,* Sam lamented to himself.

Marduk's laid-back tone continued. "He could take on the face of an unknown man and assassinate the Commissioner. He could even send another suicide pilot into the building. That seems to be the fashion these days."

"Wasn't there a Nazi squadron who did that in the Second World War?" asked Margaret, with her hand on Sam's forearm.

"Uh, I don't know. Why?"

"If we knew how they got those pilots to volunteer for that mission, we might be able to figure out how Schmidt was planning to arrange something similar. I might be way off, but shouldn't we at least investigate the possibility? Dr. Gould might even be able to help us."

"She is confined to a hospital in Mannheim at the moment," Sam said.

"How is she doing?" Marduk asked, still feeling guilty that he had hit her.

"I have not seen her since I had her admitted. That was why I came to see Dr. Fritz in the first place," Sam replied. "But you're right. I may as well see if she can help us – *if* she is conscious. God, I hope they can help her. She was in a bad way when I last saw her."

"Then I would say a visit is in order, for more than one reason. And Lieutenant Werner and his friend Kohl?" Marduk inquired, taking a sip of his coffee.

Margaret's phone rang. "It's my assistant." She smiled proudly.

"*You* have an *assistant*?" Sam teased. "Since when?" She answered Sam in a whisper just before she took the call. "I have a covert operative with a penchant for police radios and locked lines, my boy." With a wink she answered the call, walking away over the immaculate lawn lit by garden lamps.

"So, a hacker," Sam mumbled with a chuckle.

"Once Schmidt has the mask, one of us will have to intercept him, Mr. Cleave," Marduk said. "I vote you storm the wall while I wait in ambush. You flush him out. After all, with this face I will never be able to get into the base."

Sam drank his single malt and thought it over. "If we only knew what he was planning to do with it. Obviously, he should know the dangers of wearing it himself. I suppose he will get some lackey to sabotage the signing of the treaty."

"I agree," Marduk began, but Margaret came racing out of

the romantic garden with an expression of absolute horror on her face.

"Oh my God!" she shrieked as softly as she could. "My God, Sam! You won't believe this!" Margaret's ankles twisted under her haste as she traversed the grass patch to the table.

"What? What is it?" Sam frowned, jumping up from his chair to grab her before she could fall on the stone patio.

Wide with disbelief, Margaret stared at her two male companions. She could hardly catch her breath. When she evened out her breathing she exclaimed, "Professor Marta Sloane was just assassinated!"

"Jesus Christ!" Sam cried, dropping his head into his palms. "Now we're fucked. You do realize that this is World War III!"

"I know! What can we do now? This treaty means nothing now," Margaret affirmed.

"Where did you get your information from, Margaret? Has anyone claimed responsibility yet?" demanded Marduk, as tactfully as he could.

"My source is a friend of the family. All her information is usually dead-on. She lurks on the private security bandwidths and spends every waking moment of her day checking..."

"...hacking," Sam corrected.

She glared at him. "She checks security sites and covert organizations. That's how I usually get the news before the police are even summoned to the crime scenes or incidents," she admitted. "Minutes ago, over *Dunbar Private*

Security's red line she picked up the report. They have not even called the local police or the coroner yet, but she'll keep us posted on how Sloane was killed."

"So, it's not out on the wire yet?" Sam exclaimed urgently.

"No, but it is about to be, no doubt. The security company and the police will be filing reports before we even finish our drinks." Her eyes were tearing up as she spoke. "There goes our chance at a new world. Oh my God, they had to fuck this up, didn't they?"

"Of course, my dear Margaret," Marduk said as calmly as ever. "It's what mankind does best. Destroying anything uncontrollable and constructive. But we have no time for philosophy now. I have an idea, albeit a very far-fetched idea."

"Well, we have nothing," Margaret complained. "So be our guest, Peter."

"What if we could blind the world?" Marduk asked.

"Like that mask of yours?" asked Sam.

"Listen!" commanded Marduk, showing his first sign of emotion and sending Sam's loose tongue back behind pursed lips. "What if we can do what the media does every single day, only in reverse? Is there a way we can stop the reports from coming out and keep the world in the dark? That way, we'll have time to work out a solution and make sure the meeting in The Hague happens. With luck, we'll be able to avert the catastrophe we are no doubt facing now."

"I don't know, Marduk," said Sam, feeling dejected. "Every ambitious journalist in the world would want to be the one reporting on this for their station of their country. It's big news. There's no way our brethren of vultures will pass on a morsel like this out of respect for peace or for some moral standard."

Margaret shook her head too, affirming Sam's damning revelation. "If we could only slap that mask on someone who looks like Sloane...just to get the treaty signed."

"Well, if we cannot stop the fleet of ships from coming into shore, we'll have to remove the ocean on which they sail," Marduk presented.

Sam smiled, enjoying the old man's unorthodox thinking. He understood, while Margaret was lost and her face confirmed her confusion. "You mean, if the reports are coming out anyway, we must disable the media they use to do it?"

"Correct," Marduk nodded as always. "As far as we can."

"How on God's green earth...?" Margaret asked.

"I like Margaret's idea too," Marduk said. "If we can get the mask, we can fool the world into believing that reports of the assassination of Prof. Sloane are a hoax. And we can send in an imposter of our own to sign the document."

"It is a monumental undertaking, but I think I know just who could be crazy enough to pull off such a thing," Sam said. He grabbed his phone and pressed a letter on speed dial. He waited for a moment and then his face assumed absolute focus.

"Hey, Purdue!"

24

SCHMIDT'S OTHER FACE

"You are relieved of the Löwenhagen assignment, Lieutenant," Schmidt said firmly.

"So you found the man we're looking for, sir? Good! How did you find him?" asked Werner.

"I will tell you, Lieutenant Werner, only because I hold you in such high regard and because you agreed to help me find this culprit," replied Schmidt, reminding Werner of his need-to-know restriction. "It was remarkably surreal, actually. Your colleague called me to let me know he was bringing Löwenhagen in just an hour ago."

"My colleague?" Werner frowned, but played his role convincingly.

"Yes. Who would have thought Kohl had it in him to apprehend anyone, hey? But it is with great despair that I tell you this," Schmidt feigned his sorrow and his acting was transparent to his subordinate. "While Kohl was bringing in Löwenhagen, they were involved in a terrible crash that claimed both their lives."

"What?" exclaimed Werner. "Please say it's not true!"

His face lost all color at the news he knew was infested with insidious untruth. The fact that Kohl had left the hospital parking lot virtually minutes before him was testament to the cover-up. Kohl could never have achieved all of that in the short time it had taken Werner to get to the base. But Werner kept everything to himself. Keeping Schmidt blind to the fact that he knew all about his motive for catching Löwenhagen and the mask and the messy lie of Kohl's demise was Werner's only weapon. Military intelligence, indeed.

At the same time, Werner was truly shocked by Kohl's death. His distraught demeanor and upset was genuine as he fell back into his chair in Schmidt's office. To rub salt in his wounds, Schmidt played the contrite commander and offered him some fresh tea to absorb the shock of the bad news.

"You know, I shudder to think what Löwenhagen must have done to cause that crash," he told Werner as he paced around his desk. "Poor Kohl. Do you know how it pains me to think that such a good pilot with such a bright future lost his life because of my order to apprehend a callous and trai-torous subordinate like Löwenhagen?"

Werner's jaw clenched, but he had to keep his own mask on until it was the right time to reveal what he knew. With a shaky voice, he elected to play the victim so he could pry a little more. "Sir, please don't tell me Himmelfarb shared this fate?"

"No, no. Not to worry about Himmelfarb. He asked me to pull him out of the assignment because he could not stomach it. I guess I'm grateful for a man like you in my command, Lieutenant," Schmidt grimaced surreptitiously from behind Werner's seat. "You are the only one who has not failed me."

Werner was wondering if Schmidt had managed to obtain the mask and if so, where he was keeping it. That, however, was one answer he would not be able to simply ask for. That was something he would have to spy for.

"Thank you, sir," Werner responded. "If there is anything else you need me for, just ask."

"That is the kind of attitude that makes heroes, Lieutenant!" Schmidt sang through his thick lips as sweat moistened his thick cheeks. "For the welfare of one's country and the right to bear arms one must sometimes sacrifice great things. Sometimes giving one's life to spare the thousands one protects is part of being a hero, a hero Germany can remember as the messiah of the old ways and a man who sacrificed himself to maintain the supremacy and freedom of his country."

Werner did not like where this was going, but he could not act on his impulses without risking discovery. "I cannot agree more, Captain Schmidt. You should know. I'm sure no man gets to the rank you've attained by being a spineless runt. I hope to one day follow in your footsteps."

"You will, I'm sure, Lieutenant. And you're right. I've sacrificed much. My grandfather was killed in combat against the British in Palestine. My father died while protecting the German Chancellor in an assassination attempt during the Cold War," he projected his excuses. "But I tell you one thing, Lieutenant. When I leave a legacy, I will not only be remembered by my sons and grandsons as a nice story to tell strangers. No, I will be remembered for altering the course of our world, remembered by all Germans and therefore, remembered by global cultures and generations."*Hitler much?* Werner thought, but he acknowledged Schmidt's bullshit with fake support. "Exactly, sir! I could not agree more."

Then he noticed the emblem on Schmidt's ring, the very ring Werner used to mistake for a wedding band. Engraved in the flat gold base that crowned the top of his finger was the symbol of a supposedly extinct organization, the sigil of the Order of the Black Sun. He'd seen it before in his great uncle's house the day he'd helped his great aunt sell all her late husband's books in a yard sale back in the late 80's. The symbol had intrigued him, but his great aunt threw a fit when he asked if he could have the book.

He never thought about it again, until just now when he recognized the symbol on Schmidt's ring. The question of remaining ignorant had become difficult for Werner, because he was desperate to know what Schmidt was doing wearing a symbol that his own patriotic great aunt did not want him to know.

"That is intriguing, sir," Werner remarked inadvertently, without even considering the repercussions of his inquiry.

"What?" Schmidt asked, pulled out of his grand speech.

"Your ring, Captain. It looks like an antique treasure or some secret talisman with super powers like in the comic books!" Werner said excitedly, cooing over the ring as if it were just a beautiful piece of work. So curious was Werner, in fact, that he didn't even feel nervous in asking about the emblem or the ring. Perhaps Schmidt believed that his Lieutenant was truly entranced by his proud affiliation, but he preferred to keep his involvement with the Order to himself.

"Oh, this was given to me by my father when I turned thirteen years old," Schmidt explained nostalgically, looking at the slender, perfect lines on the ring he never removed.

"A family emblem? It looks very distinguished," Werner coaxed his commander, but he could not get the man to open up about it. Suddenly Werner's cell phone rang, breaking the spell at work between the two men and the truth. "My apologies, Captain."

"Nonsense," replied Schmidt, dismissing it cordially. "You are not on duty right now."

Werner watched the captain step outside to give him some privacy.

"Hello?"

It was Marlene. "Dieter! Dieter, they killed Dr. Fritz!" she cried from what sounded like an empty swimming pool or a shower cubicle.

"Wait, slow down, Liebchen! Who? And when?" Werner asked his girlfriend.

"Two minutes ago! J-j-just like th-that...in cold blood, for Christ's sake! Right in front of me!" she screamed hysterically.

Lieutenant Dieter Werner felt his stomach tighten up at the sound of his lover's frantic weeping. Somehow that wicked emblem upon Schmidt's ring was a portent of what was to come shortly after. Werner felt as if his admiration for the ring had in some evil way brought misfortune around him. He was remarkably close to the truth.

"What do you...Marlene! Listen!" he tried to get her to give him more information.

Schmidt heard the heightening of Werner's tone of voice. Concerned, he slowly entered the office again from outside, giving the lieutenant a questioning look.

"Where are you? Where did it happen? In the hospital?" he urged her, but she was completely incoherent.

"No! N-no, Dieter! Himmelfarb just shot Dr. Fritz in the head. Oh Jesus! I'm going to die here!" she sobbed in despair from the eerie echoing location he could not get her to disclose.

"Marlene, where are you?" he shouted.

The phone call ended with a *click*. Schmidt was still standing stunned in front of Werner, waiting for an answer. Werner's complexion had gone pallid as he shoved the phone back into his pocket.

"Excuse me, sir. I have to go. Something terrible has happened at the hospital," he told his commander, turning to leave.

"She is not at the hospital, Lieutenant," Schmidt said dryly. Werner stopped in his tracks, but did not turn around yet. By the sound of the commander's voice he expected to have the barrel of an officer's pistol pointing at the back of his skull, and he give Schmidt the honor of facing him when he pulled the trigger.

"Himmelfarb just killed Dr. Fritz," Werner said without facing the officer.

"I know, Dieter," Schmidt confessed. "I told him to. Do you know why he does everything I tell him?"

"A romantic attachment?" Werner sneered, finally shedding his false admiration.

"Ha! No, romance is for the meek of mind. The only conquest I am interested in is the domination of the meek of mind," Schmidt said.

"Himmelfarb is a fucking coward. We all knew that from the start. He creeps up the asses of anyone who can protect him or help him, because he is nothing but an inept and groveling puppy," said Werner, insulting the corporal with a genuine disdain he had always hidden out of courtesy.

"That is absolutely correct, Lieutenant," the Captain agreed. His hot breath tainted the back of Werner's head as he leaned in uncomfortably close. "Which is why, unlike people like you and the other dead people you will soon join, he *does* what he is *told!*"

Werner's flesh crawled with rage and hate, his whole being filling with frustration and serious concern for his Marlene. "So? Shoot already!" he said defiantly.

Schmidt chuckled behind him. "Sit down, Lieutenant."

Reluctantly Werner obliged. He had no choice, which infuriated a free thinker like him. He watched as the arrogant officer sat down, deliberately flashing his ring for Werner's eyes to see. "Himmelfarb, as you say, does my bidding because he is unable to grow a set of balls and stand up for what he believes in.

However, he gets the job done that I send him to do and I don't have to beg, follow up or threaten his loved ones for it. Now *you*, on the other hand, your scrotum is a bit too substantial for your own good. Don't get me wrong, I admire a man who thinks for himself, but when you cast your lot with the opposition – the enemy – you become a traitor. Himmelfarb told me everything, Lieutenant," Schmidt revealed with a long sigh.

"Maybe you're too blind to see what a traitor he is," Werner bit back.

"A traitor for the right side is, in effect, a hero. But let's leave my preferential determinations for now. I'm going to give you a chance to redeem yourself, Lieutenant Werner. Leading a squadron of fighter jets, you will have the honor of flying your *Tornado* straight into the assembly hall of C.I.T.E. in Iraq to make sure they know where the world stands on their existence."

"That is absurd!" Werner protested. "They've been keeping to their end of the cease fire agreement and have agreed to enter into trade negotiations...!"

"Blah, blah, blah!" Schmidt laughed and shook his head. "We all know the political eggshells, my friend. It's a ruse. Even if it were not – what peace would there be while Germany is just another bull in the corral?" His ring glimmered in the light on his desk as he came round the corner. "We are leaders, pioneers, powerful and proud, Lieutenant! The W.U.O. and C.I.T.E. are a bunch of bitches who wish to emasculate Germany! They want to throw us into the cage with the other slaughter animals. I say no – fucking – way!"

"It is a union, sir," Werner tried, but he only made the captain angry.

"A union? Oh, oh, 'union' as in the *Union* of Soviet Socialist Republics back in the day?" He sat on his desk right in front of Werner, lowering his head down to level of the lieutenant. "There is no growth space in a fishbowl, my friend. And Germany cannot thrive in a quaint, little knitting club where everyone chats along and give gifts over a tea set. Wake up! They are confining us to uniformity and cutting our balls off, my friend! You are going to help us undo that atrocity of – of oppression."

"If I refuse?" Werner foolishly asked.

"Himmelfarb will get some one-on-one time with sweet Marlene," Schmidt smiled. "Besides, I have already set the stage for a good *ass-whipping*, as they say. Most of the work is already done. Thanks to one of my loyal drones who *perform their duty under orders*," Schmidt shouted at Werner, "that bitch Sloane is out of the picture for good. That alone should warm the world up for a showdown, hey?"

"What? Professor Sloane?" Werner gasped.

Schmidt affirmed the news by sliding the tip of his thumb along his own throat. He laughed proudly and sat down behind his desk. "So, Lieutenant Werner, can we – can *Marlene* – count on you?

25

NINA'S TRIP TO BABEL

*W*hen Nina woke up from a feverish and painful slumber, she found that she was in a very different kind of hospital. Her bed, although adjustable in the same way as hospital beds, was cozy and decked with winter linen. It sported some her favorite design motifs in chocolate, brown, and tan. The walls were decorated with old art in Da Vinci's style and there were no reminders of drips, syringes, bed pans or any other humiliating devices Nina had loathed in her hospital room.

There was a bell button she was forced to push, because she was parched beyond comprehension and could not reach the water next to her bed. Maybe she could, but her skin was aching like brain-freeze and lightning, discouraging her from the task. A mere moment after she rang the bell an exotic-looking nurse in casual clothes entered through the door.

"Hello Dr. Gould," she greeted cheerfully in a subdued voice. "How are you feeling?"

"I feel terrible. S-so thir-sty," Nina forced. She did not even realize that she could see well enough again until she had gulped down half a tall glass of fortified water. When she had drunk her fill, Nina laid back on the soft, warm bed and looked about the room, finally laying her eyes on the smiling nurse.

"I can see almost completely right again," Nina mumbled. She would have smiled if she hadn't been so confused. "Um, where am I? You don't sound – or look – German at all."

The nurse laughed. "No, Dr. Gould. I'm from Jamaica, but I live here in Kirkwall as a full time caregiver. I was hired to look after you for the foreseeable future, but there is a doctor working very hard with his fellows to cure you."

"They can't. Tell them to give it up," Nina said in a distraught tone. "I have cancer. They told me in Mannheim when the Heidelberg Hospital sent my results through."

"Well, I am not a doctor, so I cannot tell you anything you do not already know. But what I can tell you is that some scientists do not declare their findings or patent their cures for fear of a boycott by drug companies. That is all I will say until you have spoken to Dr. Cait," the nurse advised.

"Dr. Cait? Is this his hospital?" Nina asked.

"No, madam. Dr. Cait is a medical scientist who was hired to concentrate exclusively on your illness. And this is a small clinic on the coast of Kirkwall. It is owned by Scorpio Majorus Holdings, situated in Edinburgh. Only a few know about it." she smiled at Nina. "Now let me just take your vitals and see if we can make you more comfortable and then...would you like to have something to eat? Or is the nausea still persistent?"

"No," Nina answered quickly, but then exhaled and smiled at the welcome discovery. "No, I am by no means nauseous. In fact, I'm famished." Nina laughed in a crooked way as not to aggravate the agony behind her diaphragm and between her lungs. "Tell me, how did I get here?"

"Mr. David Purdue had you flown here from Germany so that you could get specialized treatment in a safe environment," the nurse informed Nina, as she checked her eyes with a pen light. Nina lightly grabbed the nurse's wrist.

"Wait, is Purdue here?" she asked, slightly unsettled.

"No, madam. He asked me to convey his apologies to you. Probably for not being here for you," the nurse told Nina. *Yeah, probably for trying to cut my fucking head off in the dark,* thought Nina to herself.

"But he had to join Mr. Cleave in Germany for some sort of consortium meeting, so I'm afraid you're stuck with just us for now, your small team of health professionals," chimed the thin, dark-skinned nurse. Nina was fascinated by her beautiful complexion and wonderfully unique accent, halfway between a London noblewoman and a Rasta. "Mr. Cleave is apparently coming to see you in the next three days, so that is at least one familiar face to look forward to, right?"

"Aye, it sure is," Nina nodded, satisfied with that news at least.

THE NEXT DAY Nina felt decidedly better, although her eyes were not owl strength yet. Her skin was practically void of any burn or pain and she was breathing easier. She'd had a fever only once the day before, but it quickly subsided after she was given a light, green liquid that Dr. Cait jested was something they used on The Hulk before he became famous. Nina thoroughly enjoyed the humor and professionalism of the team, balancing positivity and medical science perfectly to benefit her well-being as much as possible.

"So, is it true what they say about steroids?" Sam smiled from the doorway.

"Aye, it's true. All of it. You should see how my balls have shriveled to raisins!" she jested with a matching look of amazement that had Sam laughing heartily.

Reluctant to touch her and ignite her pain, he just kissed her softly on her crown, smelling the fresh shampoo in her hair. "It is so good to see you, love," he whispered. "And those cheeks are flushing too. Now we just have to wait for a wet nose and you'll be ready to go."

Nina laughed with difficulty, but her smile persisted. Sam held her hand and looked around the room. There was a large bouquet of her favorite flowers with a big emerald-green ribbon around it. Sam found it quite striking.

"They tell me that is just part of the décor, changing the flowers every week and so on," Nina remarked, "but I know they are from Purdue."

Sam did not want to rock the boat between Nina and Purdue, especially while she still needed the treatment only Purdue could get her. On the other hand, he knew that Purdue had had no control over what he'd tried to do to Nina in those pitch-black tunnels under Chernobyl. "Well, I tried to bring you some hooch, but your staff confiscated it," he shrugged. "Bloody drunkards, the lot of them. Watch out for the sexy nurse. She shakes when she drinks."

Nina chuckled with Sam, but she figured he had heard about her cancer and that he was desperately trying to cheer her up with an overdose of pointless silliness. Since she did not wish to participate in this painful circumstance, she changed the subject.

"What is going on in Germany?" she asked.

"Funny that you should ask that, Nina," he cleared his throat and pulled his recorder from his pocket.

"Ooh, audio porn?" she joked.

Sam felt guilty about his motives, but he put on his pity face and explained, "We actually need some help with a bit of background on a suicidal Nazi squadron that apparently destroyed several bridges..."

"Aye, *KG 200*," she chipped in before he could carry on. "They reputedly wiped out seventeen bridges to prevent the Soviet forces from crossing. But that is mostly speculation, according to my sources. I only know about KG 200 because I wrote a dissertation on the influence of psychological patriotism on suicide missions in my second year post-grad."

"What is KG 200 exactly?" Sam asked.

"*Kampfgeschwader 200*," she said a bit weakly, gesturing for some fruit juice behind Sam on the table. He passed her the glass and she took minute sips through a straw. "They were designated to man a bomb..." she tried to recollect the name with her eyes to the ceiling, "...called, um, I think...*Reichenberg,* as far as I remember. But they were known as the Leonidas Squadron later on. Why? They're all dead and gone."

"Aye, that's true, but you know how we seem to run into things that are supposed to be dead and gone all the time," he reminded Nina. She could not argue that point. If anything, she knew as well as Sam and Purdue that the old world and its wizards were alive and well in the modern establishment.

"Please Sam, don't tell me we're up against a World War II suicide squad still flying their Focke-Wulfs above Berlin," she exclaimed, inhaling and closed her eyes in mock apprehension.

"Um, no," he started to ease her into the insane facts of latter days, "but remember that pilot who escaped with from the hospital?"

"Yes," she replied with a curious tone.

"What did he look like, you know, while the two of you were making your journey?" asked Sam so that he could ascertain just how far back to go before he started filling her in on everything that was going on.

"I couldn't see him. At first, when the cops called him Dr. Hilt, I thought it was that monster, you know, the one who was chasing my roomie. But I realized it was just the poor lad who got burned, probably having disguised himself as the dead doctor," she explained to Sam.

He drew a deep breath and wished he could suck on a smoke before telling Nina that she was, in fact, travelling with a shape-shifting killer who only spared her because she was blind as a bat and could not point him out.

"Did he say anything about a mask?" Sam wanted to treaded softly around the subject, hoping that she at least knew about the Babylonian Mask. But he was quite certain that Löwenhagen would not have shared such a secret randomly.

"A what? A mask? Like his mask that they put on him to avoid his tissue from becoming infected?" she asked.

"No, love," Sam replied, preparing to spill the beans on what they were involved in. "An ancient relic. The Babylonian Mask. Did he mention that at all?"

"No, he never mentioned anything about any other mask than the one they put on his face after applying the anti-biotic ointment," Nina clarified, but her frown deepened. "For Christ's sake! Are you going to tell me what this is about or not? Stop asking questions and finish playing the thing in your hand so I can hear what how deep we're in shit again."

"I love you, Nina," Sam chuckled. She had to be healing. That kind of wit belonged to the healthy, sexy, angry historian he so adored. "Alright, first off, let me just tell you the names of the men these voices belong to and what their parts in this are."

"Okay, go," she said, looking focused. "Oh, God, this is going to be a brain wrecker, so just ask if there is something you don't understand…"

"Sam!" she growled.

"Alright. Brace yourself. Welcome to Babel."

26

GALLERY OF FACES

$\mathcal{U}$nder the meager lights with dead moths in the bellies of their thick glass shades Lieutenant Dieter Werner accompanied Captain Schmidt to where he would be debriefed on the happenings of the next two days. The day of the signing of the treaty, the 31st October, was upon them and Schmidt's plan was almost due to come to fruition.

He had informed his squad of the rendezvous point to ready for the onslaught he was the architect of – an underground bunker once used by the SS in the area to accommodate their families during Allied bombings. He was about to show his chosen commander the hot point from where he would facilitate the attack.

Werner had not had any word from his beloved Marlene since that hysterical call from her that had revealed the factions and their participants. His cell phone had been confiscated to prevent him from alerting anyone, and he had been under the strict supervision of Schmidt around the clock.

"Not too far now," Schmidt told him eagerly, as they took the umpteenth turn down a small corridor that looked the same as all the others. Still, Werner tried to find identifying features where he could. Finally they came to a safe door with a digital keypad security system. Schmidt's fingers were too quick for Werner to memorize the code. Within moments he thick steel door had unlocked with a deafening clang and opened.

"Come in, Lieutenant," Schmidt invited.

As the door closed behind them, Schmidt switched on the bright, white overhead lights from a lever against the wall. The lights flickered rapidly a few times before staying on and revealing the interior of the bunker. Werner was astonished.

Communication devices lined the corners of the chamber. Red and green digital numbers flashed monotonously on the panels, in between two flat computer screens with one keyboard between them. Upon the right screen Werner saw the topographical rendition of the strike zone, the C.I.T.E. headquarters in Mosul, Iraq. Left of that screen was an identical monitor with satellite surveillance.

But it was the rest of the room that told Werner that Schmidt was dead serious.

"I knew that you knew about the Babylonian Mask and its makings before you even came to report to me, so that spares me all the time it would have taken to explain and describe all the "magical powers" it possesses," Schmidt boasted. "I know by some reach of cellular science that the workings of the mask is in fact not magical, but I'm not interested in how it works – just that it does."

"Where is it?" asked Werner, pretending to be psyched up by the relic. "I've never seen it? Will I be wearing it?"

"No, my friend," Schmidt smiled. "*I* will."

"As who? With Prof. Sloane dead you'll have no reason to assume the face of anyone involved with the treaty."

"It's none of your concern who I will be impersonating," Schmidt responded.

"But you know what will happen," said Werner, hoping to discourage Schmidt so that he could get his hands on the mask himself and get it to Marduk. But Schmidt had other plans.

"I do, but there is something that can remove the mask without incident. It is called The Skin. Regrettably, Neumand did not bother to lift this very important accessory when he stole the mask, the idiot! So I've sent Himmelfarb to breach air space and land on the secret strip eleven clicks north past Nineveh. He's to procure the Skin within the next two days so that I can remove the mask before..." he shrugged, "the inevitable."

"And if he fails?" asked Werner, amazed at the risk Schmidt was taking.

"He will not fail. He has the coordinates of the location and..."

"Excuse me, Captain, but did it occur to you that Himmelfarb could turn on you? He knows the worth of the Babylonian Mask. Aren't you afraid that he will kill you for it?" asked Werner.

Schmidt switched on the opposite light from the side of the

room where they stood. In its glare Werner was met with a wall full of identical masks. Turning the bunker into what looked like a catacomb, the wall of masks hung in their skull-shaped likenesses.

"Himmelfarb has no idea which one of these is the real one, but I do. He knows that he cannot claim the mask unless he takes his chances while applying the skin to my face to remove it, and to ensure her performs I'll have a gun to his son's head all the way in Berlin." Schmidt grinned as he admired the pieces on the wall.

"You made all these to confuse anyone trying to steal the mask from you? Genius!" Werner remarked sincerely. With his arms folded across his chest he slowly walked along the wall, trying to find any discrepancy between them, but it was practically impossible.

"Oh, I did not make them, Dieter." Schmidt abandoned his narcissism momentarily. "They were attempted replicas made by the scientists and designers of the Order of the Black Sun sometime in 1943. The Babylonian Mask was acquired by the Renatus of the Order while he was deployed in the Middle East on a campaign."

"Renatus?" Werner asked, not familiar with the rank system of the clandestine organization, as very few people were anyway.

"The leader," Schmidt said. "Anyway, discovering what it could do, Himmler immediately ordered a dozen to be engineered in similar fashion and experimented with it in the Leonidas Squad of the KG 200. They were supposed to attack two specific units of the Red Army and infiltrate the ranks by means of assuming the identities of the Soviet soldiers."

"These very masks?" Werner marveled.

Schmidt nodded. "Yes, all twelve of these. But it proved to be a failure. The scientists who had replicated the Babylonian Mask miscalculated or, well, I don't know the details," he shrugged. "The pilots instead became psychotic, suicidal and crashed their machines into various Soviet unit camps instead of performing the mission. Himmler and Hitler could not give two shits, since it was a failed operation. So the Leonidas Squad went down in history as the only Nazi kamikaze squadron ever."

Werner took it all in, trying to formulate a way in which to escape that same fate, while deceiving Schmidt into dropping his defenses for a moment. But quite honestly, with it being two days before the plan went live, it would be nearly impossible to avert catastrophe now. He knew a Palestinian pilot in the W.U.O. flying core. If he could reach her, she could stop Himmelfarb from leaving Iraqi airspace. That would allow him to concentrate on sabotaging Schmidt on the day of the signing.

The radios crackled and a big red spot appeared on the topographical map.

"Ah! There we are!" Schmidt exclaimed happily.

"Who?" asked Werner curiously. Schmidt patted him on the back and led him to the screens.

"Us, my friend. *Operation Leo 2*. You see that spot? That is the satellite lock-on of the C.I.T.E. offices in Baghdad. Confirmation for the ones I am waiting for will pinpoint the lock-on for The Hague and Berlin, respectively. Once we have all three in place, your unit will fly to the Baghdad point, while the other two units of your squadron will attack the other two cities simultaneously."

"Oh my God," Werner muttered, as he watched the pulsing red button. "Why those three cities? I get The Hague – the summit is supposed to be held there. And Baghdad is self-explanatory, but why Berlin? Are you priming the two countries for mutual counter attacks?"

"That is why I chose you as commander, Lieutenant. You are a strategist by nature," Schmidt said triumphantly.

The commander's wall mounted intercom speaker clicked and a sharp, agonizing tone of feedback ripped through the airtight bunker. Both men plugged their ears instinctively, wincing until the noise subsided.

"Captain Schmidt, this is Base Guard Kilo. There is a woman here to see you, along with her associate. Credentials say she is Miriam Inkley, British legal liaison of the W.U.O. branch in Germany," said the voice of the gate guard.

"Now? Without an appointment?" Schmidt shouted. "Tell her to get lost. I'm busy!"

"Oh, I would not do that, sir," Werner urged convincingly enough that Schmidt believed he was dead serious. Under his breath he advised the captain, "I heard she works for Lieutenant-General Meier. It's probably about the murders Löwenhagen committed and the press trying to make us look bad."

"God knows, I don't have time for this!" he replied. "Bring them to my office!"

"Should I accompany you, sir? Or do you want me to make myself invisible?" asked Werner, scheming.

"No, you have to come with me, of course," Schmidt snapped. He was annoyed with the interruption, but Werner remembered the name of the woman who'd helped them divert attention when they needed the police off their backs. *Sam Cleave and Marduk must be here then. I must find Marlene, but how?* As Werner trudged along with his commander on their way up to the office, he wracked his brain to figure out where Marlene could be held and how he could get away from Schmidt undetected.

"Hurry, Lieutenant," Schmidt ordered. Every sign of his previous pride and cheerful anticipation had now vanished and he was back in full tyrant mode. "We don't have time to waste."Werner wondered if he should not just overpower the captain and raid the chamber. It would be so easy right now. They were between the bunker and the base, under-ground, where nobody would hear the captain's cry for help. On the other hand, he knew by their arrival at the base that Sam Cleave's friend was upstairs and that Marduk probably knew by now that Werner was in trouble.

However, if he overwhelmed the chief they might all be exposed. It was a difficult decision. In the past, Werner had often found himself indecisive because the options were too few, but this time there were too many, each with equally difficult outcomes. Not knowing which of the pieces was the actual Babylonian Mask posed a genuine problem, too, and time was running out – for the whole world.

Too soon, before Werner could make up his mind between the pros and cons of the situation, the two of them had reached the stairs of the lightly-manned office building.

Werner ascended the stairs by Schmidt's side, with the occasional airman or administration staff member greeting or saluting. It would *be stupid to pull a coup now. Bide your time. See what opportunities present themselves first,* Werner told himself. *But Marlene! How will we find her?* His emotions wrestled with his reasoning while he kept a blank face in front of Schmidt.

"Just play along with whatever I say, Werner," Schmidt said through clenched teeth as they neared the office where Werner saw the reporter woman and Marduk waiting in their disguises. For a split second he felt free again, like there was hope to cry out and subdue his keeper, but Werner knew he had to wait.

Glances between Marduk, Margaret and Werner were brisk, hidden acknowledgements away from the keen senses of Captain Schmidt. Margaret introduced herself and Marduk as two aviation lawyers with extensive experience in political sciences.

"Please sit down," Schmidt offered, pretending to be pleasant. He tried not to stare at the strange, old man who accompanied the stern, extroverted female.

"Thank you," Margaret said. "We wished, actually, to speak to the *real* commander of the Luftwaffe, but your guard said that Lieutenant-General Meier was out of the country."

She struck that offensive nerve elegantly and with a deliberate intent to rile the captain up just a bit. To the side of the desk Werner stood stoically, trying not to laugh.

27

SUSA OR WAR

*N*ina's eyes were frozen on Sam's as she heard the last of the recording. He was afraid at one point that she had ceased her breathing as she listened, frowned, concentrated, gasped and cocked her head throughout the entire soundtrack. When it had finished, she just kept staring at him. In the background, Nina's TV was on the news channel, but mute.

"Fucking hell!" she exclaimed suddenly. Her hands were riddled with needles and tubes from the day's treatment, otherwise she would have buried them in her hair in astonishment. "You mean to tell me, the guy I thought was Jack the Ripper is actually Gandalf the Grey and my pal who slept in the same room as me and traveled miles with me was a coldblooded killer?"

"Aye."

"Why didn't he kill me as well, then?" Nina wondered out loud.

"Your blindness saved your life," Sam told her. "The fact that you were the only person who couldn't see that his face belonged to someone else must have been your saving grace. You were no threat to him."

"I never thought I'd be happy to be blind. Jesus! Can you imagine what could have happened to me? So where are they all now?"

Sam cleared his throat, a trait Nina had by now learned meant that he was uncomfortable with something he was struggling to formulate, something that would otherwise sound insane.

"Oh for fuck's sake," she exclaimed again.

"Look, this is all a long shot. Purdue is busy rounding up a group of hackers in every major city to interfere with satellite broadcasts and radio signals. He wants to prevent the news of Sloane's death from spreading too fast," Sam explained, not having much hope in Purdue's plan of stalling the global media. He was hoping, however, that it would considerably impeded, at least, by the vast network of cyber spies and technicians Purdue had at his fingertips. "Margaret, the woman's voice you heard, is still in Germany right now. Werner was supposed to notify Marduk when he managed to get the mask back from Schmidt without Schmidt's knowledge, but they had not heard from him by the deadline."

"So then he's dead," Nina shrugged.

"Not necessarily. It just means he hasn't been successful in getting the mask," Sam said. "I don't know if Kohl can help him get it, but he looks like a bit of a flake to me. But because Marduk had not heard from Werner, he went with Margaret to the Büchel base to see what is happening."

"Tell Purdue to speed up his work with the broadcast systems," Nina told Sam.

"I'm sure they are moving as fast as they can."

"Not fast enough," she contested, nudging her head at the television. Sam turned to find that the first major broadcaster had obtained the report Purdue's people had been trying to stop.

"Oh my God!" Sam exclaimed.

"This is not going to work, Sam," Nina admitted. "No news agent will care if they unleash another world war by spreading the news of Professor Sloane's death. You know how they are! Careless, greedy humans. Typical. They would rather scramble to get the credit for tattling than to consider the consequences."

"I wish I could get some of the big newspapers and social media posters to cry hoax," said Sam, frustrated. "It would be a 'he said- she said' for long enough to hold off actual calls to war.

The image on the television disappeared suddenly and some 80s music videos came on. Sam and Nina wondered if it was the work of the hackers, taking what they could get in the meantime to procrastinate more reports.

"Sam," she said at once in a gentler, sincere tone. "What Marduk told you all about the skin thing that can remove the mask – does he have it?"

He had no answer. He had not thought to ask Marduk more about it at the time.

"I have no idea," Sam answered. "But I cannot risk calling him on Margaret's phone at the moment. Who knows where they are behind enemy lines, you know? It would be a daft move that could cost everything."

"I know. I was just wondering," she said.

"Why?" he had to ask.

"Well, you said that Margaret had this idea about someone using the mask to take on the guise of Professor Sloane, even just to sign the peace treaty, right?" Nina recounted.

"Aye, she did," he affirmed.

Nina sighed hard, contemplating what she was about to bring to the table. Ultimately it would serve a greater good than just her welfare.

"Can Margaret get us in touch with Sloane's office?" Nina asked, as if she was ordering a pizza.

"Purdue can. Why?"

"Let's set up a meeting. The day after tomorrow is Halloween, Sam. One of the biggest days in recent history and we cannot let it be run into the ground. If Mr. Marduk can get the mask to us," she explained, but Sam started shaking his head profusely.

"Absolutely not! There is no way I am letting you do that, Nina," he protested vehemently.

"Let me finish!" she cried as loud as her sore body could

handle. "I'll do it, Sam! It is my decision and my body - my fate!"

"Really?" he shouted. "And what about the people you will leave behind if we don't manage to get the mask off before it takes you from us?"

"What if I don't, Sam? The entire globe descends into the fucking World War III? One person's life...or the whole planet's children under air raids again? Fathers and brothers on the front lines again and God knows what else they will use technology for this time!" Nina's lungs were working overtime to get the words out.

Sam just shook his bowed head. He didn't want to admit that it was the best thing to do. If it were any other woman, but not Nina.

"Come on, Cleave, you know it's the only way," she said, as the nurse came rushing in.

"Dr. Gould, you cannot exert yourself like that. Please leave, Mr. Cleave," she demanded. Nina did not want to be rude to the medical staff, but there was no way she was leaving this matter unresolved.

"Hannah, please let us finish this discussion," Nina implored.

"You can hardly breathe, Dr. Gould. You are not allowed to excite your nerves and send your heart rate through the roof like this," Hannah reprimanded.

"I understand," Nina replied quickly, keeping her tone cordial. "but please just allow Sam and I a few more minutes."

"What is wrong with the television?" Hannah asked, perplexed by the constant broadcast interruptions and ghosting of the images. "I'll get maintenance to have a look at our antenna." With that she left the room, giving one last look back at Nina to impress what she'd said. Nina nodded in return.

"Good luck fixing that aerial," Sam smiled.

"Where is Purdue?" Nina asked.

"I told you. He is busy linking up satellites under his umbrella companies' operations to the remote access of his clandestine accomplices."

"I mean, *where* is he? Is he in Edinburgh? Is he in Germany?"

"Why?" asked Sam.

"Answer me!" she demanded, scowling.

"You did not want him anywhere near you, so now he is staying away." Now it was out. He had said it, unbelievably defending Purdue to Nina. "He is seriously contrite about what happened in Chernobyl and you treated him like shit in Mannheim. What do you expect?"

"Wait, what?" she snapped at Sam. "He tried to kill me! Do you understand the level of distrust that cultivates?"

"Aye, I do! I do. And keep your voice down before Nurse Betty comes in again. I know what it is like to be plummeted into despair, my life threatened by those I trusted. You cannot possibly believe that he would ever deliberately want to harm you, Nina. For Christ's sake, he *loves* you!"

He stopped, but it was too late. Nina was disarmed, for what it was worth, but Sam already regretted his uttering. The last thing he needed to remind her of was Purdue's unrelenting pursuit of her affection. Already Sam was in many ways inferior to Purdue, in his own opinion. Purdue was a genius with charm to match, independently wealthy with a legacy of holdings, estates and technologically advanced patents. His reputation was stellar as explorer, benefactor and inventor.

All Sam had was a Pulitzer and several other awards and commendations. Apart from three books and a bit of money from his share in Purdue's treasure hunts, Sam had a penthouse apartment and a cat.

"Answer my question," she said plainly, observing the sting in Sam's eyes at possibly losing her. "I promise to play nice if Purdue gets me in contact with the W.U.O. head office."

"We don't even know if Marduk has the mask yet,.." Sam was grabbing at straws to mar Nina's advance.

"That's fine. Until we know for sure we may as well arrange my representation of the W.U.O. at the signing, so that Prof. Sloane's people can arrange logistics and security accordingly. "After all," she sighed, "with a petite brunette showing up with or without Sloane's face, it would be easier to cry hoax at the reports, right?"

"Purdue is at Wrichtishousis as we speak," Sam surrendered. "I'll get hold of him and tell him about your proposal."

"Thank you," she replied gently, while the television screen blinked between channels by itself, settling briefly on test signals. Suddenly it stopped on a global news station that had not been rendered powerless yet. Nina's eyes were glued to the screen. She was ignoring Sam's morose silence for the moment.

"Sam, look!" she exclaimed and lifted her hand with difficulty to point to the television. Sam turned around. The reporter appeared with her microphone with the C.I.T.E. offices in the Hague behind her.

"Turn it up!" Sam cried, grabbing at the remote control and pressing a myriad of incorrect buttons before getting the volume increased in escalating green bars upon the high definition screen. By the time they could hear what she was saying she was three sentences into her speech.

"...here at the Hague, following reports of Professor Marta Sloane's alleged assassination yesterday at her holiday residence in Cardiff. The media has been unsuccessful in confirming these reports, as the Professor's spokesperson has been unavailable for comment."

"Good, at least they are still unsure about the facts," Nina remarked. The report continued from the studio where the newscaster added more information on another development.

However, in light of the approaching summit for the signing of the peace treaty between the Meso-Arabian states and the W.U.O. the office of Meso-Arabia's leader, Sultan Yunus ibn Meccan had announced a change of plan.

"Aye, here it comes now. Fucking war," Sam growled as he sat listening in anticipation.

"The Meso-Arabian House of Representatives has altered the agreement to have the treaty signed in the city of Susa, Meso-

Arabia, following threats against the life of the Sultan by association."

Nina drew a deep breath. "So now it's Susa or war. Now do you still think my wearing of the Babylonian Mask is not pivotal to the future of world as a whole?"

28

MARDUK'S BETRAYAL

*W*erner knew he was not allowed to leave the office while Schmidt was talking to the visitors, but he had to find out where Marlene was being kept. If he could get hold of Sam, the journalist could use his contacts to trace the call she'd made to Werner's cell phone. He was especially impressed by the legal jargon flowing expertly from the mouth of the British journalist while she beguiled Schmidt with her impression of a lawyer from the W.U.O. head office.

Suddenly Marduk interrupted the conversation. "My apologies, Captain Schmidt, but may I please use your gents' room? We were in such haste to come to your base with all these fast developing matters that I admit I neglected my bladder."

Schmidt was only too helpful. He did not want to put forward a bad image to the W.U.O., as they were currently in control of his base and his superiors. Until he'd fulfilled his flaming coup of their authority he had to comply and kiss ass as far as necessary to keep up appearances.

"Of course! Of course," Schmidt replied. "Lieutenant Werner, would you please escort our guest to the men's room? And remember to ask...*Marlene*...for clearance to the B-block, alright?"

"Yes, sir," Werner replied. "Please come with me, sir."

"Thank you, Lieutenant. You know, when you reach my age, constant toilet visits are compulsory and drawn out. Cherish your youth."

Schmidt and Margaret chuckled at Marduk's remark as Werner followed in Marduk's tracks. He took note of Schmidt's subtle, encoded warning that Marlene's life was at stake if Werner tried anything out of his sight. They left the office at a slow pace to emphasize the ruse to win them more time. As soon as they were out of earshot, Werner pulled Marduk aside.

"Mr. Marduk, please, you have to help me," he whispered.

"That is why I'm here. Your failure to contact me and that less than effectively hidden warning from your superior gave it away," Marduk replied. Werner stared at the old man in admiration. It was unbelievable how perceptive Marduk was, especially for someone his age.

"My God, I love sharp people," Werner finally said.

"So do I, son. So do I. And on that note, did you at least find out where he keeps the Babylonian Mask?" he asked. Werner nodded.

"But first we have to secure our absence," Marduk said. "Where is your infirmary?"

Werner had no idea what the old man was up to, but he'd

learned by now to keep his questions to himself and to watch things unfold. "This way."

TEN MINUTES later the two men stood in front of the digital keypad of the chamber where Schmidt kept his twisted Nazi dreams and relics. Marduk sized up the door and the keypad. On closer inspection, he realized that it would be harder to break in than he'd initially imagined.

"He has a back-up circuit that alerts him if anyone tampers with the electronics," Marduk told the Lieutenant. "You will have to go and distract him."

"What? I can't do that!" Werner whispered and shouted at the same time.

Marduk foiled him with that incessant tranquility. "And why not?"

Werner said nothing. He could very easily distract Schmidt, especially in the presence of the lady. Schmidt would hardly raise a stink with her in their company. Werner had to concede that it was the only way to get the mask.

"How will you know which mask it is?" he finally asked Marduk.

The old man did not even bother with an answer. It was so obvious that, as keeper of the mask, he would recognize it anywhere. All he had to do was turn his head and look at the young lieutenant. "Tsk tsk tsk."

"Okay, alright," Werner admitted it was a stupid question. "Can I use your phone? I have to get Sam Cleave to run a trace on my number."

"Oh! I'm sorry, son. I do not have one of those. When you get upstairs, use Margaret's phone to contact Sam. Then cause a genuine emergency. Say, fire."

"Of course. Fire. Your thing," Werner remarked.

Ignoring the younger man's dig, Marduk explained the rest of the plan. "As soon as I hear the alarm I will unlock the keypad. Your captain will have no choice but to evacuate the building. He won't have time to come down here. I'll meet you and Margaret outside the base, so make sure you stick with her at all times."

"Got it," Werner said. "Margaret has Sam's number?"

"They are, as they say, 'trauchle twins' or something of that sort," Marduk frowned, "but in any event, yes, she has his number. Now go and do your thing. I shall wait for the signal of chaos." There was a hint of a jest in his tone, but Werner's face was filled with utmost focus for what he was about to endeavor.

Although Marduk and Werner had secured an alibi at the infirmary for taking so long, the discovery of the back-up circuit called for a new plan. Werner used it, however, to aid him in a believable story for when he should arrive at the office and find that Schmidt had already alerted security.

In the opposite direction from the corner where the Base Infirmary entrance was marked, Werner slipped into an administration archive room. Successful sabotage was imperative, not only for Marlene's rescue, but for practically saving the world from another war.

IN THE SMALL corridor just outside the bunker, Marduk

waited for the alarm to go off. Agitated, he was tempted to attempt fiddling with the keypad, but he refrained from it to avoid getting Werner caught prematurely. Marduk had never thought the theft of the Babylonian Mask would cause this much open hostility. Usually he could manage to eradicate thieves of the mask quickly and surreptitiously, returning to Mosul with the relic without much interference.

Now, with the political stage being so fragile and the motive behind the most recent theft being world domination, Marduk believed it was inevitable for things to get out of hand. Never before had he had to resort to breaking into places, deceiving people, or even showing his face! Now he felt like a government operative – with a team, no less. He had to admit that it felt good to be accepted as part of a team for the first time in his life, but he was just not the type – or the age – for such things.The signal he had been waiting for without warning. Red lights above the bunker started flashing as a visual silent alarm. Marduk used his technological knowledge to override the patch he'd recognized, but he knew that it would send an alert to Schmidt without the alternative password. The door opened, revealing to him the bunker filled with old Nazi artifacts and communication devises. But Marduk was not there for anything other than the mask, the most destructive relic of all.

Just as Werner had told him, he found the wall lined with thirteen masks, each of which resembled the Babylonian Mask with uncanny accuracy. Marduk ignored the subsequent intercom calls for evacuation as he checked each relic. One by one he examined them with his impressive sight, prone to scrutinize details with the intensity of a raptor. Each mask looked like the next, a slender skull-shaped covering with a dark red interior that teemed with the composite engineered by wizards of science from a cold and cruel era that could never be allowed to repeat itself.

Marduk identified the cursed mark of those scientists, adorning the wall behind the electronic technology and communication satellite controls.

He scoffed derisively, "Order of the Black Sun. It is time for you to set beyond our horizons."

Marduk took the genuine mask and slipped it under his coat, zipping up the large, interior pocket. He had to hurry to join up with Margaret and hopefully Werner, if the boy had not been shot yet. Before he exited into the reddened illumination of grey cement in the subterranean corridor, Marduk halted to survey the hideous chamber one more time.

"Well, I'm here now," he sighed laboriously, while gripping between his two palms a steel pipe from the cabinet. In just six blows, Peter Marduk destroyed the power grids of the bunker, along with the computers Schmidt was using to mark the territories bound for attack. The power outage, however, was not restricted to the bunker, but was actually tied-in to the administrative building of the air base. A complete blackout ensued all over Büchel Air Base, sending the staff into a frenzy.

After the world had seen the television report of Sultan Yunus ibn Meccan's decision to change locations for the signing of the peace treaty, the general consensus was that a world war was looming. While the alleged assassination of Prof. Marta Sloane was still unclear, it was still cause for concern by all citizens and militaries globally. Peace was

PRESTON WILLIAM CHILD

about to be established by two ever-warring factions for the
first time, and the event in itself was apprehensive at best for
most of the world's spectators.

Such restlessness and paranoia was the order of the day
everywhere, therefore having a blackout at the very air base
where an undisclosed airman had crashed a fighter jet mere
days before, was cause for panic. Marduk had always
enjoyed the chaos of stampeding people. The confusion
always lent a certain lawlessness and disregard for protocol
to the situation, and this served him well in his need to
move undetected.

He slipped up the stairwell to the exit that led onto the quad
where the barracks and administrative buildings met. Flash-
lights and generator powered troopers lit up the vicinity in a
yellow spray light that penetrated every reachable corner of
the air base. Only the mess hall sections were dark, yielding
a perfect path for Marduk to take on his way through the
secondary gate.

Regressing to a convincingly slow limp, Marduk finally
made his way through the rushing military staff, where
Schmidt shouted orders for pilots to be on stand-by and
security personnel to lock down the base. Marduk soon
reached the gate guard that had first announced him and
Margaret when they had arrived. Looking decidedly
pathetic the old man asked the frantic guard, "What is
happening? I've lost my way! Can you help? My colleague
strayed from me and..."

"Yes, yes, yes, I remember you. Please just wait at your vehicle, sir," the guard said.

Marduk nodded cooperatively. He looked back one more time. "Have you seen her pass by here, then?"

"No, sir! Please, just wait in your vehicle!" the guard shouted, as he listened for orders in the wail of alarms and searchlights.

"Okay. See you then," Marduk answered as he made his way to Margaret's car, hoping to find her there. The mask pressed against his protruding rib cage as he quickened his gait toward the car. Marduk felt accomplished and even at peace as he got into Margaret's rental car with the keys he'd lifted off her.

As he drove off with the pandemonium in his rear view mirror, Marduk felt a weight lift from his mind, an utter relief that he could now return to his homeland with the mask retrieved. What the world did with its perpetually crumbling control and power plays was of little concern to him anymore. As far as he was concerned, if the human race had become so arrogant and filled with a lust for power that even the prospect of harmony erupted into callousness, perhaps extinction was long overdue.

29

PURDUE'S RUNNING TAB

*P*urdue was reluctant to speak to Nina in person, so he stayed at his mansion, Wrichtishousis. From there he continued to orchestrate the media blackout Sam had asked for. But the explorer was by no means becoming a reclusive pity party on legs just because his former lover and friend, Nina, had shunned him. In fact, Purdue had some plans of his own concerning the imminent trouble that was beginning to rear its head over the Halloween Day horizon.

Once he had his network of hackers, broadcast experts, and semi-criminal activists cued onto the media block, he was free to initiate his own plans. His work had been marred by his personal issues, but he had learned not to allow matters of emotion to influence the more tangible tasks. In his second story study, surrounded by checklists and travel documents, he received a Skype alert. It was Sam.

"And how are things over in Casa Purdue this morning?"

Sam asked. His voice carried cheer, but his face was dead serious. Had this been a mere telephone call, Purdue would have thought Sam was the epitome of joviality.

"Great Scott, Sam," Purdue had to exclaim when he saw the bloodshot eyes and baggage on the journalist. "I thought I was the one who doesn't sleep anymore. You look worse for wear in a very alarming way. Is it Nina?"

"Oh, it is always Nina, my friend," Sam replied, sighing, "but not just in the way she usually drives me nuts. She's cranked it up a level this time."

"Oh my God," Purdue muttered, preparing for the news by sucking in a mouthful of black coffee that had gone horribly awry since its heat had withered. He winced from the sandy taste, but was more worried about Sam's call.

"I know you don't want to have to deal with anything concerning her right now, but I have to implore that you at least help me brainstorm around her proposal," Sam said.

"Are you in Kirkwall now?" asked Purdue.

"Aye, but not for long. Did you listen to the recording I sent you?" Sam asked wearily.

"I did. It is absolutely fascinating. Are you going to pursue it for the Edinburgh Post? I believe Margaret Crosby solicited you after I left Germany." Purdue chuckled, inadvertently tormenting himself with another gulp of rancid caffeine. "Blegh!"

"I thought about it," answered Sam. "If it were merely about the murders at the Heidelberg Hospital or corruption at the Luftwaffe's high command, aye. It would have been a good step toward maintaining my reputation. But that is of secondary weight now. The reason I ask if you learned the secrets of the mask is because Nina wants to put it on."

Purdue's eyes shimmered in the brightness of the screen, turning a moist grey as he glared at Sam's image. "Excuse me?" he said without flinching.

"I know. She asked that you contact the W.U.O. and get Sloane's people to adapt an...arrangement of sorts," Sam explained in a drained tone. "Now, I know you are pissed at her and all..."

"I am not *pissed* at her, Sam. I just need to distance myself from her for both our sakes – hers and mine. But I do not engage in juvenile silent treatment just because I'm taking a break from someone. I still consider Nina my friend. And you, for that matter. So whatever the two of you might need me for, the least I can do is listen," Purdue told his friend. "I can always decline if I think it's a bad idea."

"Thank you, Purdue," Sam exhaled in relief. "Oh, thank God you have more reason than she does."

"So she wants me to use my affiliation with Prof. Sloane's financial administration to pull some strings, right?" the billionaire asked.

"Right," Sam nodded.

"And then? Does she know that the Sultan has requested a change of location?" Purdue asked, picking up his cup but realizing in time that he did not want what was in it.

"She knows. But she is adamant on taking Sloane's face to get the treaty signed, even smack in the middle of ancient Babylonia. The problem is obtaining the Skin to get it off afterwards," Sam said.

"Just ask that Marduk fellow from the recording, Sam. I was under the impression you were in touch?"

Sam looked upset. "He's gone, Purdue. He was going to infiltrate the Büchel Air Base with Margaret Crosby to get the mask back from Captain Schmidt. Lieutenant Werner was supposed to as well, but he failed..." Sam took a long pause, as if he had to force out his next words. "So we have no idea how to find Marduk to borrow the mask for the signing of the treaty."

"Oh my God," Purdue exclaimed. After a short quiet spell he asked, "How did Marduk leave the base?"

"He took Margaret's rental car. Lieutenant Werner was supposed to flee the base with Marduk and Margaret after they'd obtained the mask, but he just left them there and took her c...ah!" Sam realized at once. "You genius! I'll text you her details for a trace on the car too."

"Always a thread through technology, old cock," Purdue bragged. "Technology is the nervous system of God."

"Quite possibly," Sam agreed. "It is the pages to knowing... and now I know all this because Werner called me less than 20 minutes ago, also asking for your help." In saying all of this Sam couldn't shake the guilt he felt for laying so much on Purdue after his efforts were so unceremoniously rebuked by Nina Gould.

Purdue was amused, if anything. "Wait just a second, Sam. Let me get my notes and a pen."

"Are you running a tab?" Sam asked. "If not, I think you should. I feel bad, man."

"I know. And you look like you sound too. No offence,"

Purdue said.

"Dave, you can call me dog shit right now and I wouldn't care. Just please say you can help us with this," Sam begged. His big dark eyes looked droopy and his hair unkempt.

"Now, what must I do for the lieutenant?" Purdue asked.

"When he returned to base he learned that Schmidt had sent Himmelfarb, one of the men in the recording gone turncoat, to capture and hold his lady friend. And we should care about her because she was Nina's nurse in Heidelberg," Sam explained.

"Okay, points for the lieutenant's lady friend, named?" asked Purdue, pen in hand.

"Marlene. Marlene Marx. They had her call Werner after they killed the doctor she'd assisted. The only way we can locate her is through a trace on her call to his cell phone."

"Got it. Will forward the information to him. Text me his number."

On the screen, Sam was already shaking his head. "No, Schmidt has his phone. I'm texting you his number for the trace, but you can't contact him there, Purdue."

"Oh, shit, of course. I'll forward it to you, then. When he calls, you can give it to him. Okay, so let me get on these tasks and I'll contact you soon with the results."

"Thank you so much, Purdue," Sam said, looking exhausted, but grateful.

"No problem, Sam. Give the Fury a kiss for me and try not to get your eyes scratched out." Purdue smiled as Sam chuckled mockingly back at him before disappearing in a blink of blackness. Purdue was still smiling well after the screen had gone blank.

30

DESPERATE MEASURES

*E*ven though the media broadcasting satellites were mostly dysfunctional across the board, there were still some radio signals and internet sites that had managed to infect the world with the plague of uncertainty and exaggeration. On the remaining social media profiles that could not yet be locked, people conveyed the panic of the current political climate, along with the reports of assassinations and threats of World War III.

By the corruption of servers in the major centers of the planet, people everywhere naturally came to the worst conclusions. According to some, the internet was under assault by a mighty faction of everything from aliens about to invade earth to the Second Coming. Some of the more dimwitted thought that the FBI was responsible, somehow deeming it more helpful to national intelligence to 'make the internet crash'. And so every country's citizens took to all that was left to show their discontent – the streets.

Major cities were inundated with riots, and mayoral offices

had to account for the communication embargo, which they could not. At the top of the W.U.O. tower in London, a distraught Lisa looked down on a bustling city full of discord. Lisa Gordon was second in command of the organization that had recently lost its leader.

"My God, just look at that," she said to her personal assistant as she leaned against the window pane of her 22nd Floor office. "Human beings are worse than wild animals as soon as they have no leaders, no teachers, nor any emissary with authority. Have you noticed?"

She watched the looting from a safe distance, but still wished she could talk sense into them all. "Once the order and leadership of countries falters even slightly, citizens think that destruction is the only alternative. I've never been able to understand that. There are just too many different ideologies begotten by fools and tyrants." She shook her head. "We're all speaking different languages while at the same time trying to live together. God help us. This is Babel all over."

"Dr. Gordon, the Meso-Arabian Consulate is on Line 4. They need confirmation for Professor Sloane's appointment at the Sultan's palace in Susa tomorrow," the personal assistant said. "Shall I still use the excuse that she is ill?"

Lisa turned to face her assistant. "Now I know why Marta used to bemoan having to make all the decisions. Tell them she will be there. I'm not shooting this hard-earned endeavor in the foot yet. Even if I have to go there myself and beg for peace, I will not let this pass because of terrorism."

"Dr. Gordon, there is a gentleman on your main line. He has a very important proposal for us regarding the peace treaty," the receptionist said, peeking around the door.

"Hayley, you know we do not take calls from the public here," Lisa reprimanded.

"He says his name is David Purdue," the receptionist added reluctantly.

Lisa swung around. "Put him through to my desk immediately, please."

After hearing Purdue's suggestion that they use an impostor to take the place of Prof. Sloane, Lisa was more than a little taken aback. Of course, he had not included the ludicrous use of a mask to assume the woman's face. That would have been a tad too macabre. Still, the suggestion of a changeling rattled the sensibilities of Lisa Gordon.

"Mr. Purdue, much as we at the W.U.O. Britain appreciate your ongoing generosity toward our organization, you have to understand that such an act would be fraudulent and unethical. And as I am sure you understand, those are the very methods we oppose. It would make hypocrites of us."

"I do, of course," Purdue replied. "But think about it, Dr. Gordon. How far would you bend the rules to achieve peace? Here we have a sickly woman – and have you not been using illness as a scapegoat to avert confirmation of Marta's death? And this lady, who has an uncanny resemblance to Marta, is offering to mislead the right people for but a moment in history to establish your organization within its chapters."

"I – I w-would have to...think about it, Mr. Purdue," she stammered, still unable to make up her mind.

"You had better hurry, Dr. Gordon," Purdue reminded her. "The signing is tomorrow, in another country, and time is running out."

"I shall contact you as soon as I have spoken to our advisers," she told Purdue. Internally, Lisa knew it was the best solution; no, the only one. The alternative would just be far too costly and she had to forcefully weigh her morals against the greater good of all. It was really no contest. At the same time, if she were to be discovered plotting such deception, Lisa knew she would be held accountable and probably indicted for treason. Forgery was one thing, but to be a knowledgeable accessory to such a political travesty – they would have her tried for nothing short of a public execution.

"Are you still there, Mr. Purdue?" she cried out suddenly, looking at her desk phone system as if it displayed his face.

"I am. Shall I make the arrangements?" he asked cordially.

"Yes," she affirmed firmly. "And this must never, ever surface, do you understand?"

"My dear Dr. Gordon. I thought you knew me better than that," Purdue replied. "I will send Dr. Nina Gould and a body guard to Susa on my private jet. My pilots will use W.U.O. clearance under the assumption that the occupant is indeed Prof. Sloane."

After they ended the call, Lisa found her demeanor somewhere between relieved and terrified. She paced around her office with her shoulders hunched and her arms folded tightly, contemplating what she had just agreed to. Mentally she was checking all her bases, making sure each was covered with a plausible excuse in case the charade came to light. For the first time was happy about the media delays and persisting blackouts, having no idea that she was in cahoots with the people responsible.

31

WHO'S FACE WOULD YOU WEAR?

*L*ieutenant Dieter Werner was relieved, apprehensive, but nonetheless elated. He'd contacted Sam Cleave from a prepaid phone he'd acquired while on the run from the air base, marked as deserter by Schmidt. Sam had given him the coordinates of Marlene's last call and he was hoping she was still there.

"Berlin? Thank you so much, Sam!" said Werner, standing in the cold Mannheim night, away from the earshot of the people at the gas station where he was filling up his brother's car. He'd asked his brother to lend him his vehicle, as the military police would be looking for his issue Jeep since he'd escaped Schmidt's clutches.

"Call me the moment you find her, Dieter," Sam said. "I hope she is alive and well."

"I will, I promise. And tell Purdue a million thanks for tracing her," he told Sam just before he hung up the call.

Still, Werner could not believe Marduk's deceit. He was upset with himself for even thinking he could trust the very man who had deceived him when he'd interviewed him at the hospital.

But for now he had to drive like hell to get to a factory called Kleinschaft Inc. on the outskirts of Berlin where his Marlene had been held. With every mile he drove, he prayed that she would be unharmed, or at the very least, alive. The holster on his hip held his private firearm, a Makarov he'd received as a gift from his brother on his twenty-fifth birthday. He was ready for Himmelfarb, if the coward still had the gall to stand and fight when he was up against a real soldier.

IN THE MEANTIME Sam helped Nina prepare for the trip to Susa, Iraq. They were due there the next day, and Purdue had already arranged the flight after getting the very furtive green light from the W.U.O. second in command, Dr. Lisa Gordon.

"Are you nervous?" Sam asked as Nina emerged from the room, splendidly clothed and groomed just like the late Prof. Sloane. "My God, you look just like her...if I didn't know you."

"I'm very nervous, but I just keep telling myself two things. It's for the good of the world and it will take all but fifteen minutes before I am done," she admitted. "I hear they've been playing the sick card with her absence. Well, they have that one spot-on."

"You know you don't have to do this, love," he told her one last time.

"Oh Sam," she sighed. "You are relentless, even when you lose."

"I see you are not in the least perturbed in your competitive nature, even by common sense," he remarked as he took her bag. "Come, the car is waiting to take us to the airport. In a few hours you will make history."

"Do we meet up with her people in London or in Iraq?" she asked.

"Purdue said they will meet us at the C.I.T.E. rendezvous in Susa. There you will spend some time with the *actual* successor of the W.U.O. reins, Dr. Lisa Gordon. Now remember, Nina, Lisa Gordon is the only one who knows who you are and what we are doing, okay? Don't slip up," he said, while they slowly walked out into the white fog that drifted through the cold air.

"Got it. You worry too much," she sniffed, adjusting her scarf. "By the way, where is the great architect?"

Sam frowned.

"Purdue, Sam, where is Purdue?" she repeated as they started driving.

"Last I spoke to him he was home, but he is Purdue, always up to something." He smiled and shrugged. "How are you feeling?"

"My eyes are almost completely healed. You know, when I listened to the recording and Mr. Marduk said that the mask wearers go blind, I wondered if that was not something he must have thought that night he visited me by my hospital bed. Maybe he thought I was Sa...Löwenhagen... masquerading as a chick."

It was not as far-fetched as it sounded, Sam figured. In fact, it could have been just so. Nina did tell him that Marduk asked her if she'd been hiding her roommate, so it may very well have been a real assumption on the part of Peter Marduk. Nina laid her head on Sam's shoulder and he bent his body uncomfortably to the side to be low enough for her to reach.

"What would you do?" she asked suddenly in the subdued hum of the car. "What would you do if you could wear anyone's face?"

"I had not even thought of that," he conceded. "I suppose it depends."

"On?"

"On how long I get to keep that person's face on," Sam teased.

"Only a day, but you don't have to kill them or die at the end of the week. You just get their face for a day and at the end of twenty-four hours it comes off and you have your own again," she whispered softly.

"I suppose I'm supposed to say that I would assume the face of some important person and that I would do good," Sam started, wondering just how honest he should be. "I should be Purdue, I think."

"Why the hell would you want to be Purdue?" Nina asked, sitting up. *Oh great. Now you've done it,* Sam thought. He thought of the genuine reasons he'd chosen Purdue, but they were all reasons he did not want to reveal to Nina.

"Sam! Why Purdue?" she insisted.

"He has everything," he replied at first, but she kept quiet and paid attention, so Sam elaborated. "Purdue can do anything. He is too notorious to be famous as a generous saint, but too ambitious to be a nobody. He is smart enough to devise miraculous machines and gadgets that can alter medical science and technology, but he is too modest to patent them and make a profit that way. Between his mind, his reputation, his contacts and his money, he can literally attain anything. I would use his face to progress to higher aims that my simpler mind, meager finances and insignificance could obtain."

He waited for a scathing review of his twisted priorities and misplaced goals, but instead Nina leaned in and kissed him deeply. Sam's heart jolted at the unpredictable gesture, but it went positively wild at her words.

"Keep your own face, Sam. You possess the one thing Purdue desires, the one thing for which all his genius, money and influence will profit him nothing."

32

THE SHADOW'S PROPOSAL

*P*eter Marduk didn't care about the developments happening all around him. He was used to people acting like maniacs, storming around like derailed locomotives whenever something beyond their control reminded them just how little power they had. With his hands in his coat pockets and his eyes alert from under his fedora, he passed through the panic stricken strangers at the airport. A lot of them were heading to their respective homes in case of a national shutdown of all services and transport. Having lived through many eras, Marduk had seen it all before. He'd survived three wars. Everything had always straightened out and rippled to another part of the world in the end. War would never stop, he knew. It would only move to another neighborhood. In his opinion, peace was a fallacy designed by those weary of fighting for what they had or jousting to win arguments. Harmony was just a myth written by cowards and religious fanatics, hoping that sowing the belief would earn them the monikers of heroes.

"Your flight has been postponed, Mr. Marduk," the check-in

clerk told him. "We expect all flights to be delayed due to the latest *situation*. There will only be flights available tomorrow morning."

"No problem. I can wait," he said, ignoring her scrutiny of his odd facial features, or rather lack thereof. Peter Marduk decided to take rest in a hotel room in the meantime. He was too old and his frame too skeletal for long periods of sitting. There would be enough of that on the flight back home. He checked into the Cologne Bonn Hotel and ordered dinner via room service. Looking forward to a well-deserved night's sleep without worry over the mask or having to curl up on a basement floor while waiting for a murderous thief was a delightful change of pace for his tired old bones.

As the electronic door locked behind him, Marduk's potent eyes saw the silhouette sitting in the chair. He had no need for much light, but his right hand slowly gripped the skull face inside his coat. It was not a difficult guess that the intruder was there for the relic.

"You will have to kill me first," Marduk said calmly, and he meant every word.

"That wish is within my reach, Mr. Marduk. I am inclined to grant that wish in an instant if you do not accede to my demands," the figure said.

"Let me hear your demands, for God's sake, so I can get some sleep. I've had no peace since yet another insidious breed of man stole it from my home," Marduk complained.

"Sit down, please. Rest. I can leave here without incident and allow you to sleep, or I can alleviate your burdens for good and still leave here with what I came for," said the intruder.

"Oh, do you think so?" The old man chuckled.

"I assure it," the other told him categorically.

"My friend, you know as much as all the others who come for the Babylonian Mask. And that is *nothing*. So blinded by your greed, you pursuits, your vengeance...whatever else you crave with the use of another's face. Blind! All of you!" He sighed as he plopped down comfortably onto the bed in the dark.

"Is that why the mask blinds the Masker?" came the stranger's question.

"Yes, I suppose its maker instilled in it some form of metaphorical message," Marduk replied as he kicked off his shoes.

"And the insanity?" inquired the intruder again.

"Son, you can ask as much information about this relic as you wish before you kill me and take it, but you will get nowhere with it. It will kill you or whomever you trick into wearing it, but there is no way around the fate of the Masker," Marduk advised.

"Not without the Skin, that is," the intruder revealed.

"Not without the Skin," Marduk agreed in slow words bordering on the dying. "That is correct. And if I die, you will never know where to find the Skin. Besides, it does not work by itself, so just give it up, son. Go on your way and leave the mask to the cowards and charlatans."

"Would you sell it?"

Marduk could not believe what he was hearing. He let out a delightful peal of laughter that filled the room like the agonizing cries of a torture victim. The silhouette did not move, nor did he take action or admit defeat. He simply waited.

The old Iraqi man sat up and switched on the bedside lamps. In the chair sat a tall, lean man with white hair and light blue eyes. In his left hand he held steady a .44 Magnum pointed right at the old man's heart.

"Now we all know that using the skin off the donor's face changes the face of the Masker," Purdue said. "But I happen to know..." he leaned forward to speak in a softer, scarier tone, "that the real prize is the *other* half of the coin. I can shoot you in the heart and take your mask, but it is *your* skin I need most."

Choking in astonishment Peter Marduk stared at the only person who had ever discovered the secret of the Babylonian Mask. Frozen in place, he glared at the European with the big gun, sitting in quiet patience.

"How much?" Purdue asked.

"You cannot buy the mask, and you certainly cannot buy my skin!" Marduk exclaimed in horror.

"Not to buy. To *rent*," Purdue corrected him, properly befuddling the old man.

"Are you out of your mind?" Marduk frowned. It was an honest question to a man whose motives he truly could not fathom.

"For the use of your mask for one week, and the subsequent removal of your facial skin to remove it within the first day, I will pay for a complete skin grafting and facial reconstruction operation," Purdue offered.

Marduk was stumped. Speechless. He wanted to laugh at the absolute absurdity of the offer and mock the idiotic principals of the man, but the more he replayed the proposal in his mind, the more sense it made to him.

"Why a week?" he asked.

"I wish to study its scientific properties," Purdue answered.

"The Nazi's tried that too. They failed horrendously!" the old man mocked.

Purdue shook his head. "My motive is pure curiosity. As a collector of relics and a scientist, I only want to know...*how*. I like my face just the way it is and I have this odd desire not to die from dementia."

"And the first day?" the old man inquired, more amused.

"A very dear friend needs to assume an important face tomorrow. It is of historical importance for a temporary peace between two long-fighting foes that she is willing to risk this," Purdue explained, lowering the barrel of the gun.

"Dr. Nina Gould," Marduk realized, speaking her name with gentle reverence.

Purdue, delighted that Marduk knew, continued, "If the world finds out that Prof. Sloane really was assassinated, they will never believe the truth: that she was killed by a German high officer's orders to frame Meso-Arabia. You know this. They will stay blind to the truth. They only see what their masks allow – tiny binocular views of a bigger picture. Mr. Marduk, I am dead serious in my offer."

After some consideration the old man sighed. "But I come with you."

"I would not have it any other way," Purdue smiled. "Here."

He tossed a written agreement on the table, stipulating the terms and the time frames for the 'item' that is never mentioned for what it is to make sure no one ever learned of the mask this way.

"A contract?" Marduk exclaimed. "Seriously, son?"

"I might not be a murderer, but I am a businessman," Purdue smiled. "Sign that accord of ours so that we can get some bloody rest. At least for the time being.

33

THE JUDAS REUNION

*S*am and Nina sat in the heavily guarded room, merely an hour before the meeting with the Sultan. She did not look well at all, but Sam refrained from prying. However, according to the staff at Mannheim, Nina's radiation exposure was not causing a terminal condition. Her breath hissed as she struggled to inhale and her eyes remained a bit milky, but her skin had healed completely by now. Sam was no doctor, but he could see that something was amiss, both in Nina's health and by her abstinence.

"You probably can't handle my breath near you, hey?" he played.

"Why do you ask?" she frowned, adjusting the velvet choker according to the pictures of Sloane that Lisa Gordon had supplied. They were accompanied by a grotesque sample that Gordon did not *want* to know about, even when Sloane's funeral director had been ordered to supply it by means of a questionable court order from Scorpio Majorus Holdings.

"You don't smoke anymore, so my fag breath must make you crazy," he pried.

"Nope," she replied, "just the annoying words that come out with that breath."

"Professor Sloane?" a female voice with a heavy accent called from the other side of the door. Sam nudged Nina painfully, forgetting how frail she was. Apologetically he held out his hands. "I'm so sorry!"

"Yes?" Nina asked.

"Your entourage should be here in less than an hour," the woman said.

"Oh, uh, thank you," Nina answered. She whispered to Sam. "My *entourage*. That would be Sloane's representatives."

"Aye."

"Also, there are two gentlemen here who say they are with your private security, along with Mr. Cleave," the woman said. "Are you expecting a Mr. *Marduk* and a Mr. *Kilt*?"

Sam burst out laughing, but held it in behind his hand, "Kilt, Nina. That would be Purdue, for reasons I'll decline to share."

"I shudder to think," she replied and called out to the woman, "That is correct, Yasmin. I have been expecting them. In fact..."

The two entered the room, shoving through big Arabian guards to get in.

"...they are *late*!"

Behind them the door closed. There were no formalities,

since Nina did not forget that clout she'd received in the Heidelberg Hospital and Sam did not forget that Marduk had betrayed their trust. Purdue picked up on it and cut it short right there.

"Come now, children. We can have group after we have altered history and managed not to get arrested, alright?"

Reluctantly they agreed. Nina kept her eyes off Purdue, not affording him the opportunity to make things right.

"Where is Margaret, Peter?" Sam asked Marduk. The old man shifted uncomfortably. He could not bear to tell the truth, even though they deserved to hate him for it.

"We," he sighed, "got separated. I could not find the lieutenant either, so I decided to abandon the whole mission. I was wrong to just leave, but you have to understand. I am so very tired of guarding this cursed mask, running after those who take it. Nobody was supposed to know about it, but a Nazi researcher studying the Babylonian Talmud came upon older texts from Mesopotamia and the lore of the Mask came into knowledge." Marduk took out the mask and held it up to the light between them. "I wish I could just be rid of it once and for all."

A sympathetic expression came over Nina's face, exacerbating her already weary look. It was easy to tell that she was far from well, but they tried to keep their concern to themselves.

"I've called her hotel. She has not returned or checked out," Sam seethed. "If anything happened to her, Marduk, I swear to Christ I will personally..."

"We have to get this done. Now!" Nina snapped them out of it with the stern announcement, "Before I lose my gall."

"She has to be transformed before Dr. Gordon and the rest of Prof. Sloane's people arrive, so how do we do this?" Sam asked the old man. Marduk responded by simply handing Nina the mask. Looking anxious to touch it, she took it from him. All she kept in mind was that she had to do this to save the peace treaty. She was dying anyway, so if the removal did not work, her deadline would just move up by a few months.

Looking at the inside of the mask, Nina winced through the tears lining her eyes.

"I'm scared," she whispered.

"We know, love," Sam said reassuringly, "but we will not let you die like this."...*like this...*

Nina had realized already that they did not know about the cancer, but Sam's choice of words was unintentionally haunting. With a straight, determined face Nina took the container that came with the pictures of Sloane and used tweezers to remove the grotesque contents from within. They all forced the task at hand to overshadow the sickening act, as they watched the patch of skin tissue from the body of Marta Sloane fall into the inside of the mask.

Curious to a fault, Sam and Purdue pushed together to see what would happen. Marduk simply watched the clock on the wall. Inside the mask, the tissue sample instantly disintegrated and across the normally bone-colored surface, the mask bled into a dark red hue that seemed to come alive. Minute ripples ran through the surface.

"Don't waste any time or it will expire," Marduk warned.

Nina caught her breath. "Happy Halloween," she said, and with a painful grimace she buried her face inside the mask.

Purdue and Sam waited anxiously to see the hellish contorting of facial muscles and the furious bulging of glands and folding skin, but they were disappointed in their expectations. Nina squealed a bit when her hands released the mask and it stayed behind on her face. Nothing profound happened at all, apart from her reaction.

"Oh my God, this is creepy! This is freaking me out!" she panicked, but Marduk came to sit next to her for some emotional support.

"Relax. What you are feeling is the fusion of cells, Nina. I believe it will burn a little from the nerve endings being stimulated, but you have to let it take form," he coaxed.

As Sam and Purdue looked on, the slim mask just reshuffled its composition to blend with Nina's face until it sank gracefully beneath her skin. Only slightly visible, Nina's features morphed into Marta's until the woman before them was the spitting image of the one in the picture.

"Un-fucking-real," Sam marveled as he watched. Purdue's mind was in overdrive on the molecular fabric of the entire transformation on a chemical and biological level.

"This is better than science fiction," Purdue muttered, as he leaned in to scrutinize Nina's face. "This is fascinating."

"And gross and macabre. Don't forget that," Nina said carefully, unsure of her ability to speak while wearing another woman's face.

"It is Halloween after all, love," Sam smiled. "Just pretend you are really, *really* good at dressing up as Marta Sloane."

Purdue nodded with a tiny smirk, but he was too preoccupied with the scientific miracle he was witnessing to do much else.

"Where is the Skin?" she asked with Marta's lips. "Please tell me you have it here."

Purdue had to answer her, whether they were in social radio silence or not.

"I have the Skin, Nina. No worries about that. As soon as the treaty is signed..." he trailed off, letting her fill in the blanks.

Shortly after, Prof. Sloane's people arrived. Dr. Lisa Gordon was a nervous wreck, but hid it well under her professional demeanor. She had informed Sloane's immediate family that she was ill and had shared the same update with her staff. Due to the condition affecting her lungs and throat, she would be unable to make her speech but would still be present to seal the accord with Meso-Arabia.

Leading the small group of press agents, lawyers, and bodyguards, she headed straight for the section marked 'Private - Visiting Dignitaries' with a knot in her stomach. It was mere minutes before the start of the historical symposium and she had to make sure everything went as planned. Entering the room where Nina was waiting with her companions, Lisa kept her game face on.

"Oh Marta, I'm so nervous!" she exclaimed as she laid eyes on the woman who had an uncanny resemblance to Sloane. Nina just smiled. As Lisa had requested, she was not allowed to speak; she needed conform to the charade in front of Sloane's people.

"Give us some privacy for a minute, alright?" Lisa told her

team. Once they closed the door, her entire disposition changed. Her jaw dropped at the face of the woman she would have sworn was her friend and colleague. "Holy shit, Mr. Purdue, you weren't kidding!"

Purdue smiled cordially. "Always good to see you, Dr. Gordon."

Lisa caught Nina up on the basics of what was needed, how to accept the announcements and so on. Then came the part Lisa had been most concerned about.

"Dr. Gould, I take it you have practiced forging her signature?" Lisa asked very quietly.

"I have. I believe I've got it down, but with the illness my hands are a bit less steady than usual," Nina responded.

"That's fine. We've made sure everyone knows that Marta is very sick and that she is suffering mild tremors while receiving treatment," Lisa replied. "That would help to account for any deviation in the signature, so God willing, we might pull this off without incident."

The press offices of all the major broadcasters had representatives at the venue's media room in Susa, especially since all satellite systems and stations had been restored miraculously since 2:15 am that morning.

When Prof. Sloane came out of the hallway to enter the meeting room with the Sultan, cameras turned in unison towards her. Flashes from long lens, high definition cameras created strobes of bright lights against the faces and clothing of the escorted leaders. Tense with focus, the three men responsible for Nina's welfare stood watching the whole affair on a monitor in the change room.

"She'll be fine," Sam said. "She even practiced Sloane's accent, just in case she had to answer any questions." He looked at Marduk. "And as soon as this is over, you and I will be looking for Margaret Crosby. I don't care what you need to do or where you have to go."

"Mind your tone, son," Marduk replied. "Keep in mind that without me, dear Nina will not be able to restore her image or maintain her life for long."

Purdue nudged Sam to reiterate the call for amicability. Sam's phone rang, disturbing the atmosphere in the room.

"It's Margaret," Sam declared, glaring at Marduk.

"See? She's fine," Marduk answered indifferently.

When Sam answered, it wasn't Margaret's voice on the line.

"Sam Cleave, I presume?" Schmidt hissed in a lowered voice. Immediately, Sam put the call on speaker for the others to hear.

"Aye, where is Margaret?" Sam asked, not wasting any time with the obvious nature of the call.

"That is none of your concern right now. Your concern is where she will be if you do not comply," Schmidt said. "Tell that bitch impostor with the Sultan to abandon her errand or else you can pick up the other bitch impostor with a shovel tomorrow."

Marduk looked shocked. He'd never intended for his actions to lead to the lovely lady's death, but now it had become a reality. His hand covered the bottom half of his face as he listened to Margaret screaming in the background.

"Are you watching from a safe distance?" Sam provoked

Schmidt. "Because if you are anywhere within my reach I will not do you the pleasure of sending a bullet through your thick Nazi skull."

Schmidt laughed with arrogant exhilaration. "What are you going to do, paper boy? Write an article to voice your discontent, slandering the Luftwaffe."

"Close," Sam replied. His dark eyes met with Purdue's. Without a word, the billionaire understood. With his tablet in his hand, he silently punched in a security code and proceeded to check the global positioning system of Margaret's phone while Sam jousted with the commander. "I will do what I do best. I will expose you. More than anyone else you will be unmasked for the depraved, power-hungry wannabe you are. You will never be Meier, pal. The Lieutenant-General is the leader of the Luftwaffe and his reputation will serve the high opinion the world will have of Germany's armed forces, not some impotent doormat who thinks he can manipulate the world."

Purdue smiled. Sam knew he had located the callous commander.

"Sloane is signing that treaty as we speak, so your efforts are pointless. Even if you killed everyone you are holding, it would not change the edict from coming into effect before you even raise your gun," Sam pestered Schmidt, secretly hoping to God that Margaret would not pay for his insolence.

34

MARGARET'S RISKY SCOOP

*T*errified, Margaret watched as her friend, Sam Cleave, infuriated her captor. She was tied to a chair and still lightheaded from the drugs he'd used to subjugate her. Margaret had no idea where she was, but from the little German she understood, she was not the only hostage kept here. Next to her was a heap of technological devices Schmidt had confiscated from his other hostages. While the corrupt commander pranced around arguing, Margaret put her childhood tricks to use.

When she was a little girl in Glasgow she used to freak the other children out by dislocating her fingers and shoulders for their entertainment. Since then, of course, she'd suffered some arthritis in her major joints, but she was pretty sure she could still manipulate the joints in her fingers. A few minutes before he'd called Sam Cleave, Schmidt had sent Himmelfarb to check on the trunk they brought with them. They'd salvaged it from the air base bunker, which had been all but destroyed by the intruders. He did not see Margaret's left hand slip from her handcuff and reach for the cell phone that had belonged to Werner while he'd been in captivity at Büchel's air base.

Stretching her neck to see, she extended her arm to take the phone, but it was just out of reach. Trying not to screw up her only opportunity for communication, Margaret nudged her chair every time Schmidt laughed. Soon she was so close that her fingertips almost touched the plastic and rubber of the phone cover.

Schmidt had finished stating his ultimatum to Sam and now all he had to do was watch the ongoing speeches before the signing of the treaty. He checked his watch, seemingly unconcerned about Margaret, now that she had been presented as leverage.

"Himmelfarb!" Schmidt shouted. "Bring the men in. Our time is short."

Six pilots, dressed and ready for deployment, came marching into the room in silence. Schmidt had his monitors displaying the same topographical maps as before, but since the destruction had Marduk left in the bunker, Schmidt had to make do with just the basics.

"Sir!" Himmelfarb and the other pilots exclaimed as they filed between Schmidt and Margaret.

"We have little to no time to blow up the German air bases marked off here," Schmidt said. "The signing of the treaty appears to be inevitable, but we shall see how long they maintain their agreement once our squadron of Operation Leo 2, blows up the W.U.O. HQ in Baghdad and the palace in Susa simultaneously."

He nodded to Himmelfarb, who retrieved the defective duplicate masks of the Second World War from the trunk. One by one, he gave each of the men a mask.

"Now, here on this tray we have the preserved tissue of a failed airman, Olaf Löwenhagen. One sample per man to be placed inside each mask," he ordered. Like machines, the uniformly dressed pilots did as he said. Schmidt checked how each man obliged before giving his next order. "Now remember, your fellow airmen at Büchel have already embarked on their mission to Iraq, so Operation Leo 2's first phase is complete. It is your duty to fulfill the second phase."

He flicked through the screens, bringing up the live broadcast of the Susa signing. "Right, sons of Germany, put on your masks and wait for my order. The moment it happens live on my screen here, I will know that our boys have bombed our targets in Susa and Baghdad. I'll then give you the order and activate Phase 2 – the destruction of Air Bases Büchel, Norvenich and Schleswig. You all know your designated targets."

"Yes, sir!" they answered in unison.

"Good, good. The next time I intend to assassinate an opinionated slag like Sloane, I will have to do it myself. Today's so-called snipers are a disgrace," Schmidt complained as he watched the pilots leave the room. They were on their way to a makeshift hangar, where they'd been concealing decommissioned flying machines from the various air bases Schmidt presided over.

～

ON THE OUTSIDE OF A HANGAR, a figure was cowering under the shade roofs of the parking area situated outside the giant discontinued factory yard on the outskirts of Berlin. He was briskly moving from one building to another, disappearing into each to see if there was any occupancy. He had reached the next-to-last working levels of the decrepit steel factory, when he saw several pilots emerge on their way to the only structure that stood out in the background of rusted steel and old, red-brown brick walls. It was odd and out of place thanks to the silver glimmer of the new steel material it had been erected with.

Lieutenant Werner held his breath as he watched half a dozen Löwenhagen's discuss among themselves the mission that would commence within minutes. He knew this was the mission Schmidt had chosen *him* for – a suicide mission in the vein of the Leonidas Squadron of WWII. When they mentioned the others going for Baghdad, Werner's heart stopped. He rushed to a place where he hoped nobody could hear him and made a call, checking his surroundings the entire time.

"Hello, Sam?"

INSIDE THE OFFICE, Margaret pretended to be asleep while trying to ascertain if the treaty had been signed yet. She had to, because according to previous narrow escapes and experience with military villains during her career, she'd learned that once a deal is made anywhere, people start dying. It was not called 'tying up loose ends' for nothing and she knew it. Margaret wondered how she could possibly defend herself against a career soldier and military leader with one hand tied behind her back – *literally*.

Schmidt was fuming, tapping his boot incessantly as he waited in agitation for his explosion to take place. Again he lifted his watch. Ten more minutes, according to his last estimation. He thought how brilliant it would have been if he could see the palace explode onto the high commission of the W.U.O. and the Sultan of Meso-Arabia just before sending out his local imps to implement the supposed revenge bombing of the Luftwaffe air bases by the enemy. The captain watched the proceedings, breathing hard and uttering his disdain with every passing moment.

"Look at that bitch!" he sneered, as they showed Sloane declining her speech as the same message slid from right to left across the CNN screen. "I want my mask! The moment I have it back I will become you, Meier!" Margaret looked for the 16th Inspector or commander of the German Air Force, but he was absent – at least from the office she was being kept.

At once she noticed movement in the hallway outside the door. Her eyes widened abruptly when she recognized the lieutenant. He was gesturing for her to hush and keep playing possum. Schmidt had something to say for every image he saw on the live news feed.

"Enjoy your last moments. Once Meier has claimed responsibility for the Iraqi bombings, I will discard his likeness. Then we'll see how much you can do with that ink-made wet dream of yours!" he cackled. As long as he went off on his rants he would not pay attention to the lieutenant sneaking in to overpower him. Werner crept along the wall where there was still some shadow cover, but he had a good six meters to go in white luminescent light before he could get to Schmidt.

Margaret thought to lend a hand. Pushing hard to the side, she suddenly toppled over and fell hard on her arm and hip. She let out a horrifying cry that gave Schmidt a serious start.

"Jesus! What are you doing?" he yelled at Margaret, about to put his boot to her chest. But he was not fast enough to avert the body propelling toward him and ramming him into the stacked table behind him. Werner slammed against the captain, instantly thrusting his fist into Schmidt's Adam's apple. The malicious commander tried to stay coherent, but Werner was taking no chances with how tough the veteran officer was.

Another swift blow to the temple with the butt of his gun finished the job and the captain fell limply to the floor. By the time Werner had disarmed the commander, Margaret was up on her feet, struggling to remove the chair leg from between her body and her arm. He rushed to help her.

"Thank God you're here, Lieutenant!" she gasped heavily as he freed her. "Marlene is in the Men's Room, tied to the radiator. They drugged her with chloroform, so she is not going to be able to run with us."

"Really?" his face lit up. "She is alive, and okay?"

Margaret nodded.

Werner looked around. "After we tie this swine up, I'll need you to come with me as quickly as you can," he told her.

"To get Marlene?" she asked.

"No, to sabotage the hangar so that Schmidt cannot send his wasps to sting anymore," he replied. "They're just waiting for the order. But without fighter jets they can do absolutely fuck-all, can they?"

Margaret smiled. "If we survive this, can I quote you for the Edinburgh Post?"

"If you help me, you get an exclusive interview of this whole debacle," he grinned.

35

SUBTERFUGE

*W*hen Nina laid her moist hand on the decree, it occurred her just what an impact her scribble on this piece of modest paper was about to make. Her heart skipped a beat as she looked up at the Sultan one last time before putting her autograph on the line. In a split second of meeting his black eyed gaze she felt his genuine amity and honest kindness.

"Go on, Professor," he encouraged her with a slow blink of reassurance.

Nina had to pretend that she was just busy practicing the signature again, otherwise she would be too nervous to do it correctly. As the ballpoint slid under her guidance, Nina felt her heart race. Just for her, they waited. The whole world held their breath just for her to finish signing. There would never be a greater honor in the world for her, even if this moment was begotten in deceit.

The moment she gracefully placed the point of the pen on the final dot in the autograph, the world applauded. Those in attendance cheered and rose to their feet. At the same time, millions of people watching via the direct feed prayed that nothing bad would happen. Nina looked up at the sixty-three-year-old Sultan. He shook her hand gently while staring deep into her eyes.

"Whoever you are," he said, "thank you for doing this."

"How do you mean? You know who I am," Nina asked with a refined smile, while actually being quite terrified of discovery. "I'm Professor Sloane."

"No, you are not. Professor Sloane had very dark blue eyes. But you have beautiful Arabian eyes, like the onyx in my royal ring. It's as if someone caught a pair of tiger eyes and put them in your face." Wrinkles formed around his eyes and his beard could not smother his smile.

"Please, Your Grace..." she implored, keeping her pose for the sake of the onlookers.

"Whoever you are," he spoke over her, "the mask you wear to me does not matter. It is not our masks that define us, but what we do with them. To me, it is what you did here that matters, you see?"

Nina swallowed hard. She wanted to cry, but it would tarnish Sloane's image. The Sultan led her to the podium with him and whispered in her ear, "Remember, my dear, what matters most is what we represent, not what we resemble."

During the standing ovation that lasted well over ten minutes Nina fought to keep upright, holding firmly onto the grip of the Sultan. She stepped up to the microphone where she had earlier declined to give a speech and everything died down gradually to a sporadic cheer or clapping. Until she started speaking. Nina kept her voice hoarse enough to remain mysterious, but she had to make the announcement. It had occurred to her that she only had mere hours to wear someone else's face and do something useful with it. There was little to say, but she smiled and said, "Ladies and gentlemen, esteemed guests and all of our friends throughout the world. My illness is impeding my voice and speech, so I shall make this quick. Due to my dwindling health issues, I would like to publicly step down..."

A grand bustle ensued throughout the makeshift auditorium in the Susa Palace from astonished spectators, but they all respected the leader's decision. She'd led her organization and most of the modern world into an era of better technology, efficiency, and discipline, without the robbing of individuality or judgment. For that she was revered, no matter what she elected to do with her career.

"...but, I am sure all my efforts will be flawlessly advanced by my successor and new commissioner of the W.U.O., Dr. Lisa Gordon. It has been a pleasure to serve the people..." Nina continued to end the announcement while Marduk waited in the change room for her.

"My goodness, Dr. Gould, you are quite the diplomat yourself," he remarked as he watched her. Sam and Purdue had left in a hurry after receiving a frantic phone call from Werner.

WERNER HAD SENT Sam a text with details on the incoming threat. With Purdue in tail, they'd rushed to the Royal

Guard and showed their clearance identification to have a word with the Meso-Arabian wing commander, Lieutenant Jenzebel Abdi.

"Madam, we have urgent intel from a friend of yours, Lieutenant Dieter Werner," Sam told the striking woman in her late thirties.

"Oh Ditti," she nodded lazily, not looking too impressed with the two mad Scots.

"He asked to give you this code. An unauthorized deployment of German fighter jets are based about twenty klicks outside the city of Susa and fifty klicks outside Baghdad!" Sam spilled it like an eager schoolboy with an urgent message for the principal. "They are on a suicide mission to destroy the C.I.T.E. headquarters and this palace under the command of Captain Gerhard Schmidt."

Lieutenant Abdi immediately shouted orders to her men and commanded her wingmen to join her in the covert desert compound to get ready for an air attack. She checked the code Werner sent and nodded in acknowledgment of his warning. "Schmidt, huh?" she sneered. "I hate that fucking Kraut. I hope Werner rips his balls off." She shook Purdue and Sam's hands, "I have to get suited. Thank you for warning us."

"Wait," Purdue frowned, "are you also engaging in air combat yourself?"

The lieutenant smiled and winked. "Of course! If you see old Dieter again, ask him why they called me 'Jihad Jenny' in the flight academy."

"Ha!" Sam chuckled as she jogged off with her team to arm

up and intercept any approaching threat with extreme prejudice. The code Werner supplied had directed them to the two respective nests from where the Leo 2 squadrons were to take off.

"We missed Nina's signing," Sam lamented.

"That's alright. It will be on every bloody news channel you can imagine over the next while," Purdue soothed, patting Sam on the back. "Now, not to sound paranoid, but I have to get Nina and Marduk to Wrichtishousis within," he checked his watch and quickly calculated the hours, travel time and elapsed time, "the next six hours."

"Alright, let's go before that old bastard disappears again," Sam grunted. "By the way, what did you text Werner while I was talking to *Jihad Jenny*?"

36

FACE-OFF

*A*fter they had freed an unconscious Marlene and carried her swiftly and quietly through the broken fence to the car, Margaret felt apprehensive as she stalked the hangar with Lieutenant Werner. In the distance, they could hear the pilots getting restless, waiting for the command from Schmidt.

"How are we supposed to disengage six F-16 looking war birds in under ten minutes, Lieutenant?" Margaret whispered, as they slipped under a loose panel.

Werner chuckled. "Schatz, you have played too many American video games." She shrugged sheepishly as he handed her a large steel implement.

"Without tires they cannot take off, Frau Crosby," Werner advised. "Please damage the tires enough to cause a nice blowout as soon as they cross that line there. I have a secondary plan, long distance."

In the office, Captain Schmidt woke from his blunt force induced blackout. He was tied to the same chair Margaret had sat in and the door was locked, confining him in his own holding place. The monitors were left on for him to watch, effectively infuriating him to a point of madness. Schmidt's insane eyes only conveyed his failure as the news feed on his screen delivered evidence that the treaty had been signed successfully and that a recent attempted air raid had been averted by the quick action of the Meso-Arabian Air Force.

"Jesus Christ! No! You could not have known! How could they know?" he whined like a child, virtually dislocating his knees trying to kick the chair in a blind rage. His bloodshot eyes stiffened through his blood-soaked brow. "Werner!"

OUT IN THE hangar Werner was using his cell phone as a homing device for a GPS satellite to locate the hangar. Margaret had done her best to slash the tires of the aircraft.

"I feel really stupid doing this old school stuff, Lieutenant," she whispered.

"So then you should stop doing it," Schmidt told her from the entrance of the hangar, toting a gun at her. He could not see Werner ducking in front of one of the Typhoons punching something into his phone. Margaret raised her hands in surrender, but Schmidt unloaded two slugs on her and she fell to the ground.

Shouting their orders, Schmidt finally initiated the second phase of his attack plan, if only for revenge. Wearing the dysfunctional masks, his men got into their aircrafts. Werner appeared in front of one of the machines, holding his cell phone in his hand. Schmidt stood behind the aircraft, moving slowly as he shot at an unarmed Werner.

But he had not considered Werner's position, nor where he'd been leading Schmidt. The slugs ricocheted off the landing gear. As the pilot fired up the jet, the afterburn he activated blew out a hellish tongue of fire, straight into the face of Captain Schmidt.

Looking down at what was left of the exposed flesh and teeth of Schmidt's face, Werner spat on him. "Now you don't even have a face for your *death mask*, you swine."

Werner pressed the green button on his phone and set it down. He quickly lifted the injured journalist on his shoulders and carried her out to the car. From Iraq, Purdue received the signal and initiated a satellite beam to hone in on the homing device, rapidly elevating the core temperature of the hangar. The result was quick and hot.

ON HALLOWEEN EVENING the world celebrated, having not the slightest idea how apt their dressing up and use of masks really were. From Susa, Purdue's private jet took off with special clearance and a military escort out of their air space to assure their safety. On board, Nina, Sam, Marduk and Purdue wolfed down a dinner while they headed for Edinburgh. There, a small, specialized team waited to apply the Skin to Nina as soon as possible.

The flat screen television kept them updated as the news unfolded.

"A freak accident at a deserted steel factory outside Berlin has taken the lives of several German Air Force pilots, including second-in-command Captain Gerhard Schmidt and Chief of the German Luftwaffe, Lieutenant-General Harold Meier. It is yet unclear what the suspicious circumstances were about..."

Sam, Nina and Marduk all speculated where Werner was and if he'd managed to get out in time with Marlene and Margaret.

"Calling Werner would be of no use. The man goes through cell phones like underwear," Sam remarked. "We'll have to wait to see if he contacts us, right Purdue?"

But Purdue was not listening. He was lying on his back in the reclining seat, head lolled to one side with his trusty tablet resting on his belly and his hands folded over it.

Sam smiled, "Look at that. The man who never sleeps is finally resting."

On the tablet Sam could see that Purdue was communicating with Werner, answering Sam's question earlier that evening. He shook his head. "Genius."

EPILOGUE

*T*wo days later, Nina had her face back, recuperating in the same cozy institution in Kirkwall where she'd been before. Marduk's facial dermis had to be peeled off and applied to the likeness of Prof. Sloane, dissolving the fusion particles until the Babylonian Mask was its (very) old self again. Macabre as the procedure was, Nina was delighted to have her own face back. Still heavily sedated for the cancer secret she shared with the medical staff, she fell asleep as Sam wandered off to get some coffee.

The old man was also healing well, occupying a bed in the same corridor as Nina. There was no sleeping on bloody sheets and tarps for him in this hospital, for which he was infinitely grateful.

"Looking good there, Peter," Purdue smiled as he looked in on Marduk's progress. "You'll be able to go home soon."

"With my mask," Marduk reminded him.

Purdue chuckled, "Of course. With your mask."

Sam came in to say hello. "I was just with Nina. She is still under the weather, but very glad to be herself again. Makes you wonder, doesn't it? Sometimes, to achieve the best the best face to wear is your own."

"Very philosophical," Marduk teased. "But I am arrogant now that I can smile and taunt with a full range of motion."

Their laughter filled the small section of the exclusive medical practice.

"So, all this time you have been the actual collector that the Babylonian Mask was stolen from?" Sam inquired, fascinated by the realization that Peter Marduk was the millionaire relic collector Neumand had stolen the Babylonian Mask from.

"Is that so strange?" he asked Sam.

"A bit. Usually wealthy collectors send private investigators and teams of recovery specialists out to get their stuff back."

"But then more people would know what this damned artifact really does. I cannot risk that. You saw what happened when just two men knew about its abilities. Imagine what would happen if the world knew the truth of these ancient items. Some things are better kept secret...masked, if you will."

"Couldn't agree more," Purdue admitted. It pertained to his furtive feelings toward Nina's alienation, but he decided to bury that away from the outside world.

"I am happy to hear that dear Margaret has survived her gunshot injuries," Marduk said.

Sam looked very proud at the mention of her. "Would you believe that she is up for a Pulitzer for Investigative Reporting?"

"*You* should be getting that one again, my lad," Purdue remarked, quite sincerely.

"No, not this time. She recorded the entire thing on Werner's confiscated cell phone! From the part where Schmidt explained the orders to his men to where he admits that he planned the hit on Sloane, even though he was at that point not sure if she ever really died. Now Margaret is renowned for the risks she took to uncover the conspiracy and the murder of Meier, et cetera. Of course, she spun it carefully so that no mention of a nefarious relic or pilots-turned-suicidal-madmen would disturb the waters, you know?"

"I'm grateful she decided to keep it secret after I abandoned her there. My God, what was I thinking?" Marduk moaned.

"I'm sure being a big shot reporter will make up for it, Peter," Sam comforted him. "After all, if you had not left her there, she would never have obtained all that footage that's now made her famous."

"Still, I owe her and the lieutenant some restitution," Marduk replied. "Next All Hallows Eve, to commemorate our adventure, I shall host a grand affair and they will be guests of honor. But it would have to be far away from my collection...just in case."

"Great!" Purdue exclaimed. "We can have it at my manor. What will the theme be?"

Marduk gave it some thought and then smiled with his new mouth.

"Why, a masked ball, of course."

END